I'll Always Walk Your Fish With You

A Novel

Maria Simon

Original Manuscript printed in Thailand 2012

Copyright © 2013 Maria Simon

All rights reserved.

ISBN-13: 978-0615901916 (Maria Simon)
ISBN-10: 0615901913

Graphic Design: Julie Simon

for my sisters and brothers,

most especially Jules

& for Bill,

who cheered the whole way

Then Jesus answer her, "O woman, great is your faith! Be it done for you as you desire." And her daughter was healed instantly.

– Matthew 15:28

One day, when I wasn't searching
Brilliantly, Love arrived
In a package I least expected
Were all the colors of my life
In that moment
My little soul clapped in victory
The journey had come full circle
And God winked at me.

Be patient towards all that is unresolved
in your heart.
Try to love the questions themselves.

Do not now seek the answers,
which cannot be given
because you would not be able
to live them.
And the point is,
to live everything.

Live the questions now.
Perhaps you will then
gradually,
without noticing it,
Live along some distant day
into the answers.

Rainer Maria Rilke

Prologue

She told me to come to the edge.

I was afraid.

"I know," she said, "but come to the edge."

I came; she pushed me.

And I flew.

PART I

Chapter 1

The girl had a secondhand copy of <u>The Alchemist</u> stuffed into the bottom of her bag. I still shake my head over that. Who would have ever guessed? It was unusually hot and muggy for that time of year, and my orange dress kept sticking to the seat. A couple dirty overhead fans were clearly not working – not that they would have been much help anyway – and I just wanted to get home. I crossed my arms over my chest and rested my head against the window. It was the end of the day, I was exhausted, and everyone on the bus could have told you the humidity was doing nothing for my hair. Just when I couldn't have felt any less attractive, time stood still.

When I think back to that evening I can still see her as she first walked onto the bus. She had a thin build and was slightly tall for an Asian girl. I remember her wrists being especially small, almost bird-like, and thinking to myself that she should really eat something. The back of her hair was cut short, like a boy's, with the exception of lighter highlights in the front. She was sporting a black heavy metal t-shirt – a memento from a concert, I assumed – three silver piercings in her left ear, one in her right, and two studs above her eye. Tribal-like tattoos ran up both her arms, and her cut nails that were once painted black were chipping. From a distance, she was the classic image of a Goth teenager going through a rebellious phase. Whether she was male or female was anyone's guess, but when I got past the outward statement and focused in on her face I saw a different picture. There was gentleness in her eyes. With both hands jammed into her pockets, she shrugged her shoulders up towards her face, giggled slightly like a little girl and asked me, "Are you the one?"

That bus ride was several years ago, yet I can still picture it as if it happened today. It's always been that way. It doesn't matter where I am or how much time has gone by, I can recall that particular memory with the same feeling and clarity as I did the first morning after it happened. I believe life gives each of us a few moments like that one; moments that are exempt from time and space, forever floating Elsewhere, and have the power to bring instant joy simply by being recalled. When I think about that night I can actually feel the muscles in my face curve upwards into a smile. My eyes soften and my chest sighs into a deep breath. Sometimes I feel like I know a bizarre and brilliant secret that Heaven shared only with me. The secret's name is Kekoa.

Kekoa is Hawaiian for "courageous one," which is brilliantly fitting since I don't know anyone else who has lived quite the life she has, and with as much grace as she's managed to grasp onto. Real courage involves finding the strength to do that which is scary, difficult, and or dangerous. It means knowingly walking into the lion's den, or in Kekoa's case, entering the darkness by herself.

The word *koa* means "warrior," which is also perfect. Kekoa's battle was not against another country or tribe, not even against another person or substance. Her constant struggle was, and always will be, with herself. She didn't choose this predicament, it was handed to her, and when most of us would have simply felt sorry for ourselves or given up, she took the high ground. Or rather, she rode the big wave. The Hawaiian gods knew what they were doing when they handed this name to her parents in a dream.

That's not to say she didn't have her dark days – because there's been plenty of those – but she always emerged from them back into the light. Sometimes she was gone for a few minutes, sometimes a day or a week, and sometimes she just never returned… at least not to those who loved her.

But she always found her way back to the light.

Kekoa was twenty-four when I first met her, though she clearly had a child-like spirit that dominated her personality. Her harmless sense of humor and immature jokes seemed like they should have clashed with her tough exterior; but instead, they helped reveal the innocence that was locked away inside her mind. It was easy to be fooled. Many people were too caught up in her piercings and tattoos to see the truth behind her mask. Had they taken the time, however, they would have seen those markings were nothing compared to the compassion and sensitivity she showed towards others.

In some ways she *was* like a child. The sun was her blanket, and the waves her playground. She found great comfort in being *out there*, away from the confinements of land and human law. It didn't matter what time of day or night, the ocean was like her second home, wrapping its waves around her in a gentle sway. Where others might find comfort in a mother's loving embrace, Kekoa found it in the water. Out there she had no fear.

Her prized board was one she'd cut and sanded herself, and was painted the same midnight black as her finger nails. When you looked closely at it, you could see the scratches and cuts which had accumulated over years of surfing, as well as a painful chip on the edge from when she wiped out near the North Shore. Her body displayed similar markings, but she never wanted to talk about those.

I'd never seen an all black board before. Usually they were white with girlie *hibiscus* flowers, or they at least had some type of tropical theme to them. But not this board. It was dark; like it was trying to send you a message. In an attempt to lighten things up a bit, I would refer to it as her B-2 bomber. She would giggle, but I know she never really thought my comment was funny.

Once when we were waxing her board in her uncle's shop, a distant look formed across her face. Whenever her eyes glazed like that I knew she had floated away for a bit. She then flipped the board over and exposed the underbelly. Very delicately etched into the black paint she had scratched a three-inch white outline of a shark. I realized it was a reminder to her of the stealth creature that quite literally lived under the surface of both the ocean waves and her own mind. With quiet thoughtfulness, Kekoa rubbed her palm over the figure, and then she whispered, "Mano."

Most people I know are scared of sharks, myself included. I have no trouble swimming in a freshwater lake or a pond, but when it comes to the ocean you can count me out. I won't even go in past my waist. Anytime I see a piece of driftwood bobbing up and down on a wave, or even just a large leaf, I freak out. My heart starts to race, and I just *know Jaws* is about to play out before my very eyes. Apparently I'm not alone in this fear.

But for the people of Hawai'i, and especially for Kekoa, sharks conjure up feelings of awe and familial connection. Kekoa was technically half Hawaiian and half Chinese, with both of her parents being half and half themselves. Using her bizarre humor, she referred to her family as The Coffee Creamers.

"Get it?" she'd ask. "Creamer; like half and half."

She'd lived most of her life on the island of O'ahu, and like many others in the islands, prayed to the gods and spirits that have been part of Hawai'i for years. These gods are an integral part of Hawaiian culture, and for many locals they are much more than marketing tools for tourists. They are personal idols and deities. Chanting and offerings of floral *lei*s are everyday occurrences throughout Hawai'i, with the hope of safety, protection, and *mana* in return. *Mana*, the spirit force that flows through every being and thing, along with *Aloha*, or deep soul-filled love, are at the heart of Hawaiian culture, and whether each individual person lives up to their meanings or not, their lives are interwoven with them daily. The people of Hawai'i are extremely spiritual.

Kekoa's favorite god was Mano, the shark god, and it turns out he was more than just an interest to her. He was a spirit she related to; a relationship dearer to her than any other. You might even say he was her best friend. Most people didn't really understand that about her. The ones who had some clue were fellow surfers who also held great respect for the shark-filled waters where they played. It was common knowledge and understanding that the ocean belonged to these awe-inspiring creatures, and Kekoa's surfer friends recognized they were simply guests in Mano's home.

But aside from these friends of hers, most others thought Kekoa was just plain weird. There's no doubt they were fascinated with her, even attracted to her, but they didn't understand her. Her easy laughter and bottle of bottomless beer made their way to any party that would grant them access. Charming jokes, sometimes even ridiculous ones, and seductive glances reeled in girls of all ages, gay or straight. Sadly, this often led to jealous men throwing more than just Kekoa's beer out the door. She never stayed down for long, though. Picking herself up from whichever floor she'd been plastered to, she usually found something like a Hello Kitty sticker on the cover band's speaker to catch her eye and make her giggle like nothing had happened.

"She's sexy," they told me, "she's tough, with no fear, but she's weird."

They could see something about her didn't add up (anyone with two cents could have figured that out), and they believed her fascination with sharks was just part of her quirky "dark side." Their observation wasn't entirely off, but then again, it wasn't even close.

Chapter 2

I've been coming to the islands every year since I graduated from high school. My family never really took traditional vacations – no Disneyland or Universal Studios – but we did start visiting Hawai'i at a point in my life when I was able to appreciate it. Sometimes I watch families who have packed up their whole troupe of children and dragged them off for a holiday and wonder how much of it the kids will remember when they are older. Our family never had to answer that question.

The islands have always held a sacredness for me ever since I can remember. Even when I was young I had a fascination with them. Though I lived on the mainland and had never seen a palm tree (plastic blow-up versions excluded), I had been exposed to what I later realized was *real Hawai'i*. I grew up in a very ordinary neighborhood outside of Seattle and spent my weekends riding bikes with the local kids. I think "riding bikes" is the same anywhere you live. The repetitive action of pedaling up and down the street, back and forth in front of the same houses, somehow never ceases to be fun. We made forts among the blackberry bushes in the vacant lots, and July 5th was always the time to finish off any unused fireworks from the night before. We must have kept some guardian angel quite busy with the number of bottle rockets and spinning bees that landed on nearby rooftops. Proudly, I can report we never burnt down a house.

Down the street from where we played was a small two-story home attached to a modest patio garden. I stumbled upon it one day while chasing my eight year old crush on a skateboard (and for the record, first love is very Real.) I saw something that afternoon that captivated me for years to come and changed my life forever. What I saw through the window of that cute little townhouse mesmerized me. I had never seen such a thing, other than on TV, and for the first time in my life I felt a place drawing me towards it. That kind of pull had never happened to me before, and it's obvious to say I kept coming back for more.

What I was watching were hula dancers. They had been practicing their dances in that little grey house, and I didn't even know it. With a fascinated eye, I started to watch their every move. I envied their ability to dance with such grace and storytelling in their hands; their fingers sculpting and drawing images in nothing but the air around them. It was breathtaking. The curve of their hips swaying back and forth was like watching waves roll. Even with Seattle's cool rain showers pounding against the windows, they were able to transport the warmth of the islands with their beautiful movements. I thought they were magical, and I wanted to be one of them.

The hula studio was owned by a native Hawaiian woman who moved to the mainland long ago. The walls were covered with tattered photographs that were fading and changing color, as well as news clippings from her life as a young island girl. The pictures revealed *lei* making contests and weddings, *luau* dancing and family celebrations – all of which reflected the same warmth as the dancers' swaying hips.

The pictures showed a whole different world, one very different from where I had been living. This place seemed like a dream, only it was real, and the people in the photos seemed like they knew a secret only they were privileged to.

Melelani, the owner of the studio, was a longtime widow who'd never had children of her own, so she lit up anytime us kids from the neighborhood put our faces up against the glass windows to sneak a peek at her hula lessons. If it had been raining earlier in the day and the windows were fogged up, we usually couldn't resist drawing smiley faces on the glass. Auntie Mele, as we referred to her, never got upset with us and instead invited us in to come sit on the floor so we could watch the girls. She loved sharing her special *"aloha spirit"* anytime should could, and it didn't end with hula. On the days when no lessons were being taught, she would lead us to her living quarters above the studio. She was famous for making homemade wontons and coconut pudding, which she never seemed to be out of. Once in a while we even got to help her make them. I loved dipping the small paint brush into the egg yolk and gently sealing the dough at the moistened edges. Auntie cooked them up in a gigantic wok, and she made us wait *forever* as they cooled on the paper towels. If I close my eyes, I can still smell the oil.

We all called Melelani "Auntie" for as long as I can remember. Everyone did, even our parents. She wasn't really that old, and actually seemed quite ageless. She was one of those women who reaches a certain age and then stays there every year after.

Comfortable in her own skin, she literally glowed with wisdom, compassion, and joy. Everyone loved Auntie Mele, for she embodied the *Aloha Spirit*.

As time went on, Auntie seemed to be teaching less and less, but she still invited us kids into her home. She told us stories about Hawaiian folklore –about Laka, the goddess of hula – and other sacred spirits of the islands. Her living room was decorated with woven baskets, hand stitched island quilts, dried flowers from *leis* that held special significance for her, and wooden *tiki* statues. I always had a special fondness for her *tikis*. These little men-like figures with scary looking mouths and extremely high foreheads possessed a sweet scent which Auntie explained was from the *koa* wood of O'ahu.

"*Koa*," she said while making a fist with her hand, "is full of strength."

I loved visiting Auntie Mele and hearing her stories. I loved staring into the faces of her *tiki* statues, cooking with her in her tiny ten-foot long kitchen, and on occasion, even dancing together. The slack-key guitar music of "Gabby" was always playing on her tape deck, and without fail, every time I saw her she would play me her favorite song. She claimed everyone knew who Gabby was (the same way I assumed everyone had heard of Madonna.) Her favorite song was titled, *Hi'ilawe*; a poetically written song, or *mele*, about two lovers and their secret love affair. Auntie's name actually meant "song from Heaven," and she claimed *Hi'ilawe* was *her* song. She would play it over and over, swaying her hips in a smooth circular motion, knees slightly bent, and her feet softly brushing along the floor back and forth. Her hands and fingers would tell the story of the two lovers being described as waterfalls and fragrant mist. I was mesmerized as I watched her. I never knew if she was thinking of her late husband or simply being taken over with emotion by the beautiful rhythm of the song. All I knew was that in those moments she was Elsewhere.

When it was my turn to dance, she draped a large piece of tropical print fabric around me, tying a strong intricate knot behind my neck. The red sheet with large yellow leaves and yellow flowers was wrapped over my clothes, which made me look a bit stupid. Honestly, I didn't really care. Long white *puku* shell necklaces, called *leis*, she draped over top, and she pinned a silk *hibiscus* flower into my hair. Auntie turned me around so I could look at myself in the mirror. I was in awe. Despite the 80's panda sweatshirt and Bongo jeans underneath, I looked like a Hawaiian princess. I smiled and looked up at Auntie Mele. She was giggling.

Chapter 3

A week before my high school graduation, Auntie invited me over to her house for a special afternoon tea. She had made lemon scones and tiny cucumber sandwiches. I thought it was all very British. Her hair was swept up into a bun at the base of her neck, and her classic silk flowers were once again pinned into place. She donned the simple lavender and white Hawaiian print dress I had seen numerous times, claiming the pattern represented Hawaiian royalty.

We talked at great length about the future, and Auntie insisted that fabulous journeys were waiting for me up ahead. I thought she was being a bit out there and dramatic, but the mysterious spirit that always hovered around my Auntie felt assuring in that moment, and so I went with it. She was forever doing that – saying something a bit off the wall, but having a look about her that was all-knowing – and she never came across as arrogant or conceited.

Instead, she would smile and shrug her shoulders, chuckle a bit and say, "I just know what I know, sweetheart."

From out of nowhere, Auntie Mele handed me a gift wrapped in lavender paper. I carefully peeled back the tape on the ends and slid out a small koa-wood box with a gold hinge along the edge. The scent of the wood was stronger than the old *tiki* figures in her living room, but it was still the same. Carefully, I lifted the lid and was amazed at what was shining back at me; so much so that I actually took in a huge breath and just held it. Staring up at me was a gold bracelet, just like Auntie Melelani's.

Auntie lifted the exquisite piece out of the box and slid it over my right wrist. It fit perfectly. Instead of being round, it was oval, wrapping around my arm much more naturally than the cheap bangles I was used to wearing. (And sadly, the "gold" on those rubbed off after about two weeks.) Looking back at me was my own name carved in gold and filled in with black enamel. The design around the back was cut in a scallop fashion, detailing *maile* leaves and *plumeria* flowers, and there was even a tiny inscription inside as well. It was beautiful. I pushed the bracelet around, trying to read behind my arm, but had trouble getting it to stay put.

Auntie took my hands, looked into my eyes and said, "You have a true love of the islands, my dear."

I didn't understand what she meant by that, and to confuse me even more, she had written the same message inside the bracelet.

Normally I have no problem talking, I even pride myself on being a natural public speaker, but this was one time when I was at a loss for words. Auntie could tell I didn't understand any of this, and to be honest, I was feeling quite overwhelmed by the gift. Never in my life had someone given me such an expensive piece of jewelry, not even my parents. The inscription didn't make much sense to me either. I wasn't Hawaiian, and I had never been to Hawai'i. What was Auntie trying to say?

She could see the confusion all across my face, and with her charming laughter she snapped me out of it. She collected my hands back into hers, our bracelets clanging next to each other, and began explaining to me that blood does not define spirit.

My entire life I had lived in Seattle, surrounded by overcast skies and endless cups of Starbucks coffee. I had never felt the warm powdery sand of Mele's childhood between my toes, nor tasted the sweetness of a fresh young coconut, and yet I understood Hawai'i better than some of her own siblings. Auntie pointed out how when I was quite young and came to visit her, the tape deck was often times paying traditional Hawaiian chats. The chanter's voice coupled with the beat of the gigantic *i'pu* mesmerized me. I would sit on the floor cross-legged and just stare at the tape deck. It was comforting to me, like the rocking of ocean waves; other times it sounded like a beating heart. As the years passed, I was able to differentiate between the voices I heard. "Uncle George" was truly my favorite. Mind you, I had no idea what the words meant unless Auntie explained them to me, and most of the time she didn't say anything. It didn't matter, though. I remember those chants feeling like they were part of a universal language, not spoken with the mouth, but felt in the heart. Some people might think chanting sounds silly, but from a small age I had a deep rooted connection to the voices coming from her boom box.

Rising from the couch, Auntie walked over to the mantel and took down a small dried *lei*. It was so small I hadn't really noticed it before. When I realized what it was, I was shocked; I couldn't believe she had kept it. The *lei* was one I had made for her a long time ago. In earlier years when Auntie's hula studio was active with dancers, they frequently strung their own *leis* using fresh flowers flown in overnight from O'ahu. One time I was at her house when the UPS box arrived.

Auntie first removed the cold pack that kept the flowers from wilting. Then she ever so gently scooped out the blossoms. She held one up to my nose for me to smell, and I loved the fragrance. I asked her if I could make a *lei* like the older girls, and of course Auntie said yes.

I went to town on what I thought was a decent *lei*, adding my own unique touches here and there. Keep in mind I was only eight at the time. I ran the 6-inch threaded needle through scented *tuberose* and *pikake* blossoms, turning them this way and that, and even threading small origami cranes between the flowers. (I was known for folding origami or biting my nails when I was bored. You can guess which one my mother preferred.) I folded a handful of tiny cranes using paper from the note pad sitting next to the phone, and figured they'd make a special design. Otherwise, I thought, all our *leis* would look the same. In the end, I was quite pleased with my little craft project. I didn't know it was worthy of being kept all these years, however.

Lei making is an art. Women who weave and string these beautiful creations have their own signature way of designing and arranging the flowers. It's not as simple as just threading a string through the petals. (Though some people do that; tourists don't know the difference.) At eight years old, I apparently designed a *lei* that seasoned *lei* makers would have smiled about. Where did I learn to do that? Auntie said I was just doing what felt natural.

And then there was the photo on her dresser. In Auntie's bedroom sat a silver frame holding a photograph of a beautiful woman wearing a Victorian gown and gold bracelets. I always thought the woman was her mother or grandmother, and one day I finally asked her. Auntie Mele's face softened; she looked reflective, even a little sad. Gently, she answered.

"No, she's not my mother, not the way you think."

I was really surprised. I thought for sure she and Auntie were related. Why else would she have this woman's picture on her dresser? (I mean, sure, I had a photo of Jonny Depp taped above my desk, and clearly he wasn't my brother.) Still, the face behind the glass seemed familiar. Auntie and I had grown really close, and maybe I just assumed that any family of hers would feel like family to me as well. Auntie Melelani had become like my fairy godmother, and it turns out Auntie had a godmother of sorts, too.

Queen Lili'uokalani was the last reigning monarch of Hawai'i. She loved her islands and her people *deeply*, and she fought hard to preserve their land before the Americans claimed it as their own. She believed in, and prayed to, a loving God, as well as honored the spirits that moved among Hawai'i. Most importantly, she was a symbol of *Aloha* for all her people. She taught them to gently say "*aloha*" from deep within, not in a loud boisterous way like many tourists do. She claimed *aloha* was the deepest form of pure love, and that when you said it to another you were actually recognizing the presence God within them. Queen Lili'u was a symbol of strength and grace, and my Auntie had the deepest respect and love for her. Auntie said Lili'u was misunderstood by her critics and instead was "bursting with *mana*."

Auntie Mele told me I reminded her of Lili'u, which really shocked the heck out of me. No, I definitely wasn't royalty, but my stubborn curiosity and care for others were apparently similar to that of Auntie's idol. I was honored by such a compliment, however, I still couldn't figure out why the Queen's picture seemed so familiar. I didn't believe in reincarnation, or anything quite so out there like that, but I did believe in the spirit world. Perhaps she'd been floating nearby.

As I admired my bracelet a little more on the couch, I suddenly had a flashback; the photo of Lili'u in Auntie's room showed her wearing gold bracelets. I ran into the room to grab the picture and sure enough, they were just like mine. Auntie Mele walked down the hallway and stood inside the doorframe. Once again, she was smiling. She came over to the bed where I was sitting and looked down at the photograph with me. Lovingly, she ran her fingers through my hair and then held my hands in hers.

"The bracelets started with her," she said, and then she proceeded to tell me the story of the first gold bangle with black enamel.

The giving of these uniquely designed gold bracelets had become a tradition among the women in Hawai'i. Mothers and grandmothers presented them to young girls in their late teenage years; a symbol of womanhood, and a celebration of the name engraved in gold.

"And so," Auntie said with a smile, "for these reasons and many others, you are more Hawaiian than any party store grass skirt or Waikiki keychain. You live *aloha* every day and you feel the spirit of the islands in your soul. One day when the time is right, you will go there and find what you didn't even know you were looking for.

"Oh, yes," she said with a twinkle in her eye. "Before I forget – a little light reading for the plane."

She handed me a brown paper bag with a book inside. It was a title I'd never heard of before.

Chapter 4

My parents decided it was time to stop and smell the roses, so they bought into a time share condo in Hawai'i. They sprung the news on me right before my commencement ceremony and said we were going to Honolulu in June. I was ecstatic! First of all, we never usually went anywhere. My parents were driven professionals who put most of their time and energy into trekking along their career paths. The fact they were making such a huge change in lifestyle was both shocking and thrilling. It was about time. Dad said a friend had "made him an offer he couldn't refuse." (He was forever quoting *The Godfather* and thinking he was funny.)

What excited me the most was the location. I was finally going to Hawai'i! For as long as I could remember, I'd been tapping my foot to the chants of the ancient Hawaiians and dressing up in shell *leis* and tropical prints. Now I was going to *really* experience what Auntie Mele called *the aloha spirit*. It was one thing to talk about Hawai'i and to dream about it, but it was a whole other to actually be there.

In the days leading up to our departure, I imagined hula girls would be waiting for me when I got off the airplane; fragrant intricate *leis* draped over their arms, and maybe even a lone ukulele player sweetly strumming this strings. Would girls be dancing on the beaches every night? Would the women all wear gold bracelets like mine? Would everyone speak to each other in loving and poetic ways like the lyrics of Gabby? Would they reflect the deep connection of *aloha* Queen Lili'u talked about?

And how about what Auntie had said? She told me Hawai'i had a gift waiting for me and somehow she was usually right.

Our flight out of SeaTac airport was scheduled to leave at 10:35am. They advised passengers to arrive two hours early for check in and boarding, but they obviously didn't know my mother. She's that woman who was forever convinced three car accidents would take place on the freeway between our house and the airport. Dad and I didn't even bother arguing or trying to talk reason with her when it came to such matters; it was a lost cause. At 7:03am, our car pulled into the airport parking lot, and all I could think about was finding a Starbucks. One good thing about the rainy city of Seattle is that we are never at a loss for coffee shops.

While my parents took care of the tickets and luggage, I plopped myself down in one of those overstuffed velvety plum colored chairs the coffee chain is famous for providing at no extra charge. I kicked off my shoes and tucked my feet underneath my legs. I was grossed out to think of how many others had probably done the same before me. But oh well. I popped the plastic lid off the green mer-person cup and waited for the initial stream to blow away before taking my first sip. Most people burn their mouths because they fail to include this crucial step in the coffee drinking ritual. What can I say – we take coffee seriously in the Pacific Northwest.

Seeing as how I had *hours* to kill before our flight took off (and no, there hadn't been any accidents on the road that morning,) I figured I would take a look at the book Auntie had given me the week before. I had tucked it in my backpack, knowing I would need something to help me pass the time; the small paperback novel didn't look like it was going to be rocket science. I flipped through the pages quickly and figured I could probably finish the whole thing before even landing in Honolulu. I didn't know anything about the story, but knew Auntie wouldn't suggest something unless she thought it was worthwhile. I picked up my coffee and took a sip, and then I opened to the first page. I began reading and didn't leave the velvety chair until ten minutes before boarding.

Normally I would have been excited about the novelties of flying. Yes, I'm that person. I'm all about the in-flight movie, endless cans of soda, and most importantly, the adorable small food containers. But I hardly even noticed them on this trip; I couldn't put down my book.

The story quickly flowed from one page to the next. I was flipping pages so often that Dad even gave me a look a few times. Before I knew it, I was staring at the epilogue. What a beautiful little story, I thought; so simple and yet so deep. There were passages that seemed like they were written just for me, though I knew they weren't, really. The charming tale about a boy in search of his treasure was obviously supposed to mean something to me about my own life. I just didn't know what exactly. I decided not to worry about it because right outside my window at that very moment I could see turquoise water leading up to the coast of O'ahu.

Our plane touched down smoothly in Honolulu, and I felt like my heart was going to burst. It was beating out of control with excitement. I was about to experience the full flood of tropical paradise all around me and deep rich culture everywhere I turned. I just knew it. I stood up tall and smiled as we entered the airport so the hula girls would feel at ease when they presented me with my *lei*. I confidently walked through security and paused – there were no girls waiting at the gate to welcome me, and the *leis* were going to cost $10.

I was crushed. I was beyond disappointed. My first impression of Hawai'i was not at all living up to my love of the culture. I followed my parents out of the air-conditioning to the queue of taxis waiting to take tourists in ridiculous hats to their beach front hotels. The smile that had once been on my face when we exited the plane was now dipping into a slight frown.

I was trying not to tear up when a gentle breeze blew through my hair; a scent sweeter than lavender or roses awakened my senses. I actually tilted my head upwards and closed my eyes. The air was warm and fragrant, and it didn't seem to be in any kind of hurry. Ignoring the tourists, I looked around me at the men who drove the taxis and were helping to organize the queue. They wore colorful shirts and bright smiles. There was joy in their faces and laughter in their voices as they joked with one another and greeted their customers. They reminded me of Auntie Mele. The wind blew a little stronger, knocking a few of the newly bought hats to the ground. (I swear those hats looked like they were made out of whicker.) Watching dutiful husbands chasing after such monstrosities actually made me chuckle. Looking around, I took in a really deep breath, inhaling the perfume of jasmine *leis* and *plumeria* blossoms from the tree above me. A single thought went through my mind: somehow this felt like home.

Chapter 5

The great thing about owning a time-share condo with workaholics is that you pretty much get to have the place to yourself whenever you want it. At least that was the case for me. The spacious two-bedroom condo my parents bought into sat idly most of the year. No one was taking advantage of the ocean view and two minute walk to the beach. Therefore, I felt it was my duty to put the place to good use. God did not create beauty to then have it be ignored.

Getting there was a bit of a bumpy road, however. After graduating from high school, I decided to take some time away from studying. I mean honestly, thirteen years of education had been enough for awhile. I wanted to have a bit of freedom and time to clear my head, and to figure out what I really wanted to do with the next chapter of my life.

There's seriously too much academic pressure on teens these days, and it starts the first day of freshman year. I had to map out my whole four-year plan and pick the right classes from day one if I wanted any kind of chance at a decent college or university. Extra years of science and math, as well as learning to say "could you please pass me an egg?" in a language I was never going to use again had become standard minimums. Honors classes, advanced placement classes, and college courses taught in the high school were just a few of the other gems. I'm not even going to get into the SATs. A check-off list of extracurricular activities was supposed to mean we were well rounded and worldly. Athletics, band, leadership camp, volunteer club, church group, the possibilities were endless. Who needed that kind of stress?

The worst part about the whole deal was it didn't guarantee anything. I watched classmates have complete breakdowns because they didn't get accepted to their parent's alma mater. You would have thought someone died the way they carried on. In all fairness, I understood the pressure they were under, and when you're seventeen these kinds of blows seem like atomic bombs. It was painful to watch. (Except when it happened to a certain pompous cheerleader who thought daddy could buy her anything. I'm, of course, not naming any names.)

My folks were really cool about the whole thing. I'd been a decent student all four years, averaging a 3.65 overall GPA. But as senior year was coming to a close, I was getting burnt out. Just the thought of sitting in more classes made me depressed. I had no desire to move into a dorm and share a six foot block of space with a complete stranger, and I definitely had no idea what I wanted to study. I couldn't even narrow down which school I wanted to attend. (Unlike a certain senior I know, I *was* accepted to my parent's alma mater, and it had nothing to do with who my father was.)

Dad proposed we take a road trip to check out the three schools I'd been accepted to. Perhaps walking on the campus would do the trick. Because of my parents' crazy careers, we had never done the father/daughter campus visits before now. Most of my friends had gone and checked out schools, some even in their junior year, and they told me it would make a world of difference. Campus tours and overnight dorm stays had become their preferred weekend activity. I, however, didn't even know where to begin. It was hard to get a true sense of these places from their brochures and websites. I mean they all seemed to be "not too big/not too small," "committed to diversity," and apparently blessed with sunny days 365 days out of the year.

We gave it our best shot; I was even optimistic. Really, I was. But I failed to get that warm glow or special fuzzy feeling my friends had talked about. Nothing really clicked, and I didn't get a sense of "home" when I walked among the brick buildings and Frisbee throwing students. (No offense to the overly friendly tour guides who obviously adored their schools.) But I just wasn't feeling it. This frightened me, actually. What in the world was I going to do?

Dad never laughed at me though, and he obviously wasn't worried about it as much as I was. He tried to make me feel better by suggesting we stop off at the outlets on our way home. This was coming from a man who despised shopping. It made me smile; he was really trying. We walked into The Gap, and I headed towards the mark down section. Ace of Base was singing "All That She Wants," and "cantaloupe" had apparently been named color of the season.

After a few minutes, I looked around and tried to figure out where my dad had disappeared to when I saw him checking out the accessories. He was pretending to look interested in banana clips while bobbing his head up and down and tapping his foot to the beat. (Oh my goodness – he was trying to be cool!) If buying new clothes didn't make me feel better, watching my father was definitely going to take care of it. As I was making my way through the clearance rack, Dad came over and put his arm around me. (His head was still bobbing.) In that loving way daddies sometimes do with their little girls, he gave my shoulder a squeeze and said a little time off might be just the thing to help me recharge before I tried to "get back in the saddle." (Oh yeah, he also liked quoting from *Top Gun*.)

A big weight had been lifted. When we returned home and shared the news with mom, I was pleasantly surprised to find her supportive, too. She didn't want me sitting around watching TV all day, but taking a short break from school seemed like a viable option for the time being. She suggested I go backpacking in Europe or volunteer in Africa. She was serious. I had to give mom credit; she had come from nothing and worked her tail off to get where she was. She believed women were capable of doing whatever they wanted, and she didn't want anything keeping her daughter back. Mom was clearly a *conservative* feminist. I was still expected to one day marry a nice young man, have 2.5 children, and live happily ever after. (How exactly one is supposed to measure 0.5 children is beyond me.) She wanted me to have it all, I know that, but she didn't understand that what was right for her might not be the same thing that's right for me. Europe and Africa – though they sounded exotic and exciting, just weren't it. Both of them were half a world away and required language skills my Advance Placement class hadn't prepared me for. Japanese wasn't going to do me much good while munching on brie or scratching a mosquito bite.

We let the subject lie and decided to revisit it after graduation. When my parents told me about the condo in early June, I flipped out. It was the perfect solution. I could chill on the beach and let my worries wash away. Maybe I would even "find myself" while sipping a pina colada, complete with little umbrella, of course. I had always wanted to go to Hawai'i, mostly due to Auntie Mele's influence, but I also wanted to go because I needed to get somewhere far away and just be. (Europe and Africa were too far.) I was ready; I think we all were. We packed our bags and headed out for twenty-one days of relaxation and spectacular sunsets.

Despite my initial disappointment upon arrival at the Honolulu airport, Hawai'i managed to wrap me around its little finger. The sun, the beach, the food, you name it. My parents and I just hung out and acted like kids. Mom even willingly left her laptop in its case the days we went snorkeling. For the first time in as long as I could remember, my family played together without worrying about deadlines or final exams. Dad and I took surf lessons every day for a week (well, honestly, Dad surfed and I watched), and mom faithfully went for her daily massage with "Paul." Apparently, he was the best.

I flew through a handful of books and responsibly worked on my SPF-15 tan. We hiked Diamond Head, swung poi balls at the Cultural Center, paid our respects at the USS Arizona, and scarfed down tons of shaved ice. The days felt alive and full of energy. People smiled at one another, and it was easy to see why so many called this paradise.

But when the sun began to dip below the ocean, a wave of calm hushed over the island. This was my favorite time to be on the beach because most people had headed back to their hotels by then. It was quiet, and the waves seemed a little calmer. I would sit on the sand and look out at the great vastness of water, experiencing peace like I'd never known before. Twilight wrapped itself around me with the little light that was left, and I listened to my heart beat.

I could faintly hear chanting off in the distance, and I seriously thought I was making it up the first night it happened. But then I squinted my eyes and saw three outrigger canoes paddling by. Six to ten men were seated in each one, as their oars fell to either side of the boats. They were quite a ways out from shore, but I was still able to make out the strength in the paddlers' movements. There was only one word to describe it – *mana*.

Chapter 6

I was in love, and it wasn't with a boy. Ok, maybe I wasn't *in love*, exactly, but for the first time in a long time I fancied something deeply. Hawai'i captured my heart during those three weeks my family vacationed on O'ahu. Sometime during the last week an idea came to me. It was like an epiphany. Why not take advantage of the time share condo and enroll in some community college courses in Hawai'i? The change of scenery would do me good, and I wouldn't be wasting time just twiddling my thumbs back in

Seattle. Mom and Dad thought I was really onto something and supported my idea immensely. Personally, I think they were pleased about me still living under their roof, even if I was an ocean away.

Before we left the island, Dad and I drove over to Kapiolani Community College to pick up their course catalogue. We walked around the campus on our own (I voted not to put myself through another overly enthusiastic campus tour), and though I still didn't experience any kind of warm fuzzy feeling, I did feel content. I was relieved.

The day after I got home I went to visit Auntie Mele. I brought her coconut chips and Lion macadamia coffee – her favorites. She wanted to hear all about my vacation. I told her about the flowers and the breeze, the *luaus* and the surf lessons, and even about my disappointing welcome at the airport. She tried not to laugh.

As I began to replay the weeks for her, I suddenly realized that sitting in her modest home actually felt more exotic and real than several of the places I had just visited. It didn't really hit me until that moment that all along I had had *real* Hawai'i and *real aloha* surrounding me. I didn't need to fly across the ocean to find it.

Auntie wasn't surprised about my decision to move to O'ahu. She thought it was a splendid idea for me to bask in the sun and take some general education courses. Her only reservation was about not seeing me. I promised to write her every week, and was convinced I would be home for good after no more than a few terms. I couldn't just keep sipping mai-tais forever.

Before I left, I remembered to thank Auntie for the book she had given me. She didn't say anything and just smiled. I wrapped my arms around her and gave her a big bear hug.

"Gently," she whispered.

I jumped back, worried I had hurt her. She saw my surprised and laughed.

"I'm fine," she reassured me. "Just please remember to always be gentle with yourself."

We stood there quietly for a moment, just staring at one another; there were no words to say. But even now I can still hear her voice in my head.

"Gently."

It felt like no time had passed at all and I was back on O'ahu. My parents suggested I move over a month before classes began so I could become better acquainted with the island. I had to figure out the bus system, find a place to buy groceries, and maybe even meet a few people. I didn't have high expectations for the first month, but I did push myself to try something new each day.

On my first morning, I ventured out to a little café down from the condo for breakfast and met a lively local named Noa. He made me feel right at home; seating me at the table next to the open window and refilling my coffee twice for free. The Koi Café belonged to his family, but he found himself running the place most of the time. I told him I had just arrived the day before and planned to be around for awhile.

"Welcome to the neighborhood, sista," he said with a big smile.

I knew it was crazy – I mean, I had just met the guy – but I secretly loved the idea of having Noa as my new brother.

When I returned to the condo in the afternoon the weather began to change. A grey cloud had just hung itself over the city, and it started to downpour. Gale winds blew this way and that, while convertibles quickly put their tops up. I ran for the lobby, but didn't quite make it in time. I was drenched. Coming from Seattle, I was use to rain, but this was a different kind of storm. This felt like a monsoon. (I know I'm exaggerating, but this was beyond sprinkles.) My hair, my bags of groceries, my clothes, everything – soaked. I just wanted to cry. As I got into the elevator and looked at my pitiful reflection in the mirror, a dapper gentleman got on as well. He glanced at me and smiled; I know he felt sorry for me.

"Looks like you got caught without an umbrella," he said.

"Yep, looks like it," I snapped back. (Ok, I know that was rude, but honestly, did he have to state the obvious?)

"Why don't you let me help you out there," he continued, as he proceeded to pick up my bundle of salad fixing that were now floating in the plastic bag.

"I'm Jeffery, by the way."

Great first impression. Months later Jeffery would give me grief over that one, but at least I was able to laugh about it. That August day in the elevator, as pathetic as it was, turned out to be one of the best days of my life. Meeting Jeffery was a gift I hadn't expected.

Come to find out, Jeffery was my neighbor. He owned a condo on the 15th floor, just three above mine. For five years he had been living in Hawai'i, following his divorce from a woman he hardly ever saw. Apparently they met in graduate school and supported each other through PhDs and breast cancer. Other than that, they had lived separate lives in different towns, until one day she decided she wanted more. Their marriage of thirteen years ended civily, but Jeffery refrained from dating anyone after.

Jeffery was a shorter-sort of man, nearly as tall as me, and fit as a teenager. He had clearly been losing his hair for several years, but combed it in a way that gave his last remaining strands a sense of dignity. His clothes were always pressed and coordinated, and his gold-rimmed glasses spotless. His nails were perfectly manicured, his mustache neatly trimmed, and his British accent charming. He held the door for others, and without fail, stood when a lady entered the room. He was a proper gentleman.

After our awkward introduction in the lift, Jeffery and I continued to run into each other in the lobby and along the sidewalk leading to the complex. Two weeks had passed and I was starting to get my bearings around town when he invited me up for late afternoon tea. I hadn't really made any friends, except for Noa, who I continued to see every morning for my endless cup of coffee and papaya with lime. (Noa seriously knew what he was talking about when he said the citrus would make the fruit "pop!") Aside from him, Jeffery was the only constant in my new Hawaiian life.

"Sure, why not?" I told him when he asked me on that bright Tuesday afternoon.

We set a time for 4pm, and he told me to "simply bring myself." He would take care of the rest.

What to wear?! I mean I know it wasn't a date or anything like that, but Jeffery was probably twenty years older than me, and he was always so polite and proper. Our first interaction hadn't been the best, and I wanted to try to right the wrong. Cargo shorts and a cotton tank top were out of the question. It was time to break out a sun dress. I attempted to curl my hair, but honestly didn't know why I bothered. Between the breeze and humidity, my locks did as they pleased. Jeffery had told me not to bring anything, but I felt badly showing up empty handed. I arranged some oatmeal cookies I'd recently picked up at the market onto a paper plate. They obviously weren't homemade, but they were better than nothing.

Like most girls before an outing with someone of the opposite gender, I was primped and primed way before I needed to be. Why do we do this to ourselves? I'm dying to know if men are just as silly. I had about an hour and a half before I needed to head up to the 15th floor. I was going to drive myself crazy if I just sat there, so I decided to start writing a letter to Auntie Mele. I told her about my adventures at the flea market around the Aloha Stadium and the cheap *tiki* I purchased at the ABC minimart down the street. I had no idea what it was actually made from – it clearly wasn't real wood – nor what this *tiki's* name was. But that didn't matter to me, he was special in his own way.

I looked up at the clock and was shocked to see how the time had gotten away from me. It was

4:13. How in the world did that happen? First I was way too early, and then I was late. I told myself to relax; I was just having tea with some nice older guy from the complex. That's all. Why was I acting like a teenager on her first date?

I grabbed my newly purchased bag – another treasure from the flea market – and headed towards the elevator. The doors were just about to shut when I realized, darn it!, I had forgotten the cookies. I made a quick escape from the lift, ran back to the condo, grabbed the paper plate and rushed back out the door. By this point, the display I'd made with the cookies had turned into a landslide; broken pieces smashed against the plastic wrap. You could say it was lacking in elegance.

When Jeffery opened the door I was beyond embarrassed handing him the plate. However, he was a most gracious host, oohing and ahhing over my "oatmeal biscuits." (Damn, he's good.) He instantly complimented me on my dress and invited me into the living room. There was a stark contrast between his place and mine. The timeshare condo had a minimal amount of cheap furniture, mostly white linen and bamboo. The rooms were sparse and fairly clean, and lacking in personality, and somehow sand from the beach showed up in the most unusual of places (we'll just leave it at that.)

But Jeffery's home was filled with rich dark wood, leather chairs and walls of books. There were silver frames and carved trinkets lining his shelves and tables, and paintings that looked like they must have been expensive were hanging on the otherwise bare walls. If I didn't know better, I would have thought I'd stepped out of Hawai'i and right into London.

Jeffery could tell I was taken aback, and he started to chuckle as a smile formed on his face. The little lines under his glasses curved upwards and his eyes sparkled.

"Not what you expected?" he said in a way that was more making a statement than asking a question.

My right foot began to hide behind the back of the left one, and I felt a bit embarrassed. Was I that obvious?

Without missing a beat, and in a clear effort to easy me of my uneasiness, Jeffery gestured for us to move over next to the floor to ceiling windows that looked towards Diamond Head. The view from his condo was much better than from mine, and I must say the crater was truly majestic just off in the distance a little ways. In the course of our conversation, I found out Jeffery actually preferred the mountains to the ocean if he had to choose one. I told him that for me nothing could compare to the sea.

"Have you heard of *mana o ali'i*?" he asked.

I knew *ali'i* meant royalty, but wasn't familiar with the legend he was referring to.

"The bones of the *ali'i* are believed to be full of *mana*, even after someone has died," he told me. "They are considered so sacred that no one is allowed to know where they have been hidden in the *mauna*, the mountains."

Jeffery said every time he looked at the green hillside, he could literally feel its strength. It was the same way I felt about the waves.

Our late afternoon together was actually quite enjoyable. Once I calmed down a bit, I found myself feeling at home in Jeffery's place. We talked about how he first came to Hawai'i, and I shared about my past dilemma regarding school after graduation. We finished off a plate of scones and cucumber sandwiches, and even managed to take care of most of the oatmeal cookies. Jeffery had of course made the scones and sandwiches, and he promised to give me the recipes before I left.

I learned all about the proper way to brew and drink tea that afternoon. Before that day, tea meant taking a little bag out of a Twining's box, dropping it in a mug of hot water, and leaving it there. Proper tea service, however, involved putting a whole system in place before actually taking a sip. Jeffery had arranged a tray in the kitchen, which held a bone china pansy teapot, two pansy cups and saucers, two tiny gold spoons, a stained mesh strainer (obviously well used), a small creamer of milk, and a petite saucer of sugar cubes (adorable little tongs included). He heated up the kettle on the stove and took it off just before it started to boil.

"We don't want to burn the leaves, now do we?" (I honestly had no idea what he was talking about.)

He poured a small amount of water into the teapot and swirled it around.

"We must first warm the pot. That way it won't be shocked when we pour all the water in." (Seriously?)

"Oh right," I said, trying to sound like this was old news to me.

He then put the mesh strainer into the pot and poured a tiny bit more water over the mesh.

"Let me guess – to prepare the strainer?" I asked.

"Exactly," he said with a proud smile. I tried so hard not to roll my eyes.

He then used a silver spoon to scoop out loose leaf tea from an old fashioned English canister above the stove. He dropped the tea into the strainer and just waited a moment. My face must have revealed more than I realized because using his hand in a waving motion he explained that the steam from the recently heated mesh was "exciting" the leaves. (You have got to be kidding me.) I tried to keep my face as still as possible; I was so close to busting out laughing.

After about a minute, Jeffery poured the hot water over the tea and covered the top of the pot. We let it steep for four minutes exactly, and then he took the tea strainer out. As he picked up a long neck tea spoon, he turned to me most seriously.

"This is the vital step most people fail to include," he said.

He stirred the brewed tea about three times and then put the lid back on. With a very satisfied smile, he picked up the tray, motioned for me to head back into the living room, and stated, "Tea is served."

I sat down on the end of the brown leather couch, and Jeffery chose an end chair next to the coffee table. He poured some tea into each of the two cups and then asked my preference regarding milk and sugar.

"I'll have whatever you're having," I said, completely unsure of what was coming next.

Jeffery explained that he never used sugar in his tea, but always had it on hand for guests, and that "just a touch" of milk makes all the difference in the world. A dollop of milk was dropped into each of the paper thin china cups, and then Jeffery ever so gently used the tiny gold spoon to stir two full circles in his, being extra cautious not to let it scrape against the bottom of the cup. Only two delicate stirs of the wrist – that's all that was required. I would have swirled it around at least five times, but I tried my best to follow his lead.

Finally, I thought to myself, we can drink our tea. This ritual had already taken at least fifteen minutes, and my trusty old teabags were looking better and better as time ticked by. I was just about to pick up my cup and take a gulp when I noticed the delicate and precise way Jeffery was holding the handle. I had already put my pointer finger through the loop, since that was the only way I could secure the cup from falling out of my hand. I mean, isn't that what the hole is for? But Jeffery had a whole different set up going on. He didn't even bother with the loop, and instead used his pointer finger and his thumb, simply pinched together, to hold the cup. (Are you kidding me?!)

Life has a really funny way of humbling all of us. This was another one of those moments. I attempted to mimic Jeffery's actions, pinching the edge of the handle in a ladylike fashion. Very slowly, I began to lift from the saucer towards my lips. The cup wobbled a bit, and I saw the tea slosh up along the edge like a wave crashing into a sea wall. But miraculously it stayed inside the cup as I kept my back straight like the ladies in an Agatha Christie novel. Jeffery sipped away and kept up his end of the conversation. I made a little more progress moving the cup closer to its final destination when all of a sudden I completely lost control of the cup. Before I knew it, my wrist had given out, the slightly creamed tea was all over the coffee table, and my face was bright red. I could have died.

But once again, Jeffery saved the day. Without wasting a moment on concern for his furniture, he quickly reassured me.

"Oh don't you just hate that? That happens to me all the time with these particular cups. The handles are just way too small for any practical tea drinking fingers. Here, let me get you a dampened cloth."

He jumped up and returned from the kitchen in no time. It all happened so fast that I hardly had time to move. Jeffery had managed to clean up the spilt tea, pour two more cups, dropped in the dollops of milk, and began the next part of our conversation without me even saying a single word. He acted like what had just taken place was the most normal and common occurrence in the world. I could have kissed him for that.

I was still embarrassed forty-five minutes later when we were finishing the last of the sandwiches, but since Jeffery never mentioned the accident again, I didn't either. Instead, I actually felt myself relax and even started laughing a bit when he told me about the first time he attempted a surf lesson. Let's just say it wasn't really his thing.

The sun eventually started to set to the right of Diamond Head, and I decided that was my cue to start heading home. Before I left, I walked over to the walls of bookcases and took a peak at some of the titles. There were books I'd never heard of, some in old leather binding, and there were also bestsellers from the last couple of years. To my surprise, tucked in between James Baldwin and Kahlil Gibran was the same little book Auntie Mele had given me right before graduation.

"Have you read this?" I asked as I pulled it off the shelf. Jeffery just grinned and paused.

"Have you?" was his reply.

"Yeah – right after graduation. My Auntie gave me a copy before I flew to Hawai'i for the first time. It's a great little read."

Jeffery took a deep breath and sipped the last drops of tea from his cup.

"You should read it again," was all he said, and then he picked up the finished tea service and took it into the kitchen.

What was that all about, I wondered? I didn't waste much thought on it, and followed him into the other room. He was writing down the recipe for the scones, as promised, and asked if I wanted to take the remaining oatmeal cookies back with me. I laughed a little.

"Really, I insist, they're all yours."

"You know, books are meant to be savored, not tossed aside after one read," Jeffery said as he continued to write out the scone recipe. "Every time I re-read a story, I fall into a deeper layer of what the author is trying to say. The simplest of sentences can leave the most profound impact."

"I guess I can see your point," I said while watching him put the cap back on his Mont Blanc pen. I realized he was quite serious about what he was saying. He relaxed his shoulders, sat back on the stool, and let out a long exhale before he continued to share.

"Dear, I can't tell you how many times I have read the same books over and over again, and each time when I come to certain passages my eyes tear up. You would think by now I would know it's coming. But instead, every time the words hit me like a first kiss. In that moment, the whole world opens up, everything makes perfect sense, and I'm left speechless."

I had never thought about a book like that before, and Jeffery continued to look at me for what felt like longer that it probably was.

"The same thing can happen when you meet someone new," he finally said.

I wasn't sure how to take that last comment and decided it was my cue to leave. I thanked him for the lovely afternoon, and he said the pleasure was all his. He also told me not to be a stranger. I promised I wouldn't, and when I was just about to reach for the doorknob, Jeffery lifted my right hand and brushed it with his lips.

"Until next time," he said.

PART II

Chapter 7

I was surprised at how quickly I fell into a normal routine. Before I knew it, the sound of palm branches blowing against each other when a breeze picked up didn't faze me. The sweet melodies that were piped through speakers in every corner of every store started to sound familiar. And if I hadn't known better, I would have thought I'd been eating papaya with fresh lime squeeze over top my whole life.

My mornings down at Noa's café became a daily habit. He usually had a few good stories to tell me about his adventures the night before when he was out with "his boys." Other times he just went off about the "sweetest wave" he'd experienced on his board that very morning. Noa usually hit the waves right before the sun rose, getting in a couple hours of surfing before having to take care of the coffee shop. He was one of those guys who was probably a lot older than he looked, but had such amazing energy and enthusiasm for life that he seemed ageless. Even if it was raining outside – which I secretly missed – breakfast at the Koi Café felt full of sunshine.

I also continued to see Jeffery. We had several more tea parties, routinely met for lunch, and even had a couple movie nights. *Out of Africa* was his pick; *The Hours* was mine. We always found ourselves knee deep in conversations that went on and on. Before we knew it, the time would get away from us and it would be well past midnight. Jeffery was just so easy to talk to, despite our significant age difference; he was unlike anyone else I'd ever known. His stories were full of rich tapestry and minute detail. His words were never rushed, and neither were his gestures. Clearly, he was quite particular about how he did things, and every belonging had its own place. But what I adored the most about him were his eyes – the way they looked right through me, like he knew something about me that even I didn't know – and I adored his voice.

More than a few times I caught myself holding my breath when Jeffery and I stared at each other, and I had the same reaction when I heard him talking down the hall. It was like a drug. When he spoke, there was a combination of deep emotion and gentle strength about each word that passed his lips. It was soothing, and yet powerful. It calmed me and excited me all at the same time. And before I knew it, I was falling for him.

At first I thought I was crazy. I couldn't be in love with a man who was technically old enough to be my father. But I was. Age had nothing to do with it, and obviously sex had nothing to do with it either. I guess some people will just love you for the sole purpose of loving you, and that's what this was: it *was* love – a kind of love I had never experienced before.

It was gentle and kind, engaging and intellectual. It was nothing like the teenage novels I had read in high school, nor like the movies Jeffery and I watched together. But it was definitely there, and it was definitely Real. What I was supposed to do about it, however, I had no idea.

Chapter 8

Every morning when I woke up, Jeffery was the first thought on my mind. I wondered if he was up yet, and if so, what he was doing. Clearly, I had fallen for him; it was pretty obvious. I thought about what he might be eating for breakfast – whether he made scones with tea or ate cornflakes like me when I was too lazy to make it down to Noa's for coffee. (My money was on the scones.) The morning sun started looking brighter and softer. The days seemed happier and I became giddy. Sometimes I would get so excited just at the *thought* of running into him in the hall that I would catch myself smiling when I was all alone. Once I even dropped my bag when I was trying to get myself out the door – all because I was thinking of Jeffery.

But then I actually *would* see him, and that would bring on a whole new level of ridiculous behavior. I laughed way too easily at anything he said (making me sound like a ditz. But I have to say, he was doing it, too.) I smiled a lot, and often times found myself at a loss for words. I couldn't think of anything to say. I was too busy looking at his eyes, imagining the feel of his arms, and listening to the way he said each word. What I loved most of all was when he said my name. Though he said it softly, I could feel his voice down in the depth of myself, right below my heart. More than once I had to put my hand on my stomach just so I wouldn't fall over. He was that powerful.

And his scent. Oh my! Don't even get me started. They say the sense of smell is the strongest of the five senses. Well, Amen to that! One whiff of his cologne made me drunk, high, excited, and mush all at the same time. I just wanted to wrap myself up it. (So I did – I went to the fragrance counter at the mall and sampled several bottles until I found the one that was his.) To this day, that scent still takes my breath away.

One afternoon, when the two of us were coming back up the elevator from having lunch down the street, I felt him step closer to me. We both stood quietly, but I could feel his breath and his chest rising and falling; it was inches away from my back. Every hair on my arms stood in anticipation, and without a moment's hesitation, I turned and looked at him. Heat was rushing through every part of my body – my face, my chest, my stomach, my legs. It felt like I was buzzing. He looked at me, swallowed, but still didn't say a word.

The elevator opened, which broke our stare and we quietly walked into the vacant hallway. Without missing a beat, Jeffery took my hand and turned me towards him. I tilted my head up, my breathing became much quicker, and I tried to brace myself. With gentle passion, Jeffery stepped into my space as I backed up against the hallway wall. Determination spread across his lips, and he cupped my face with both of his strong hands. He leaned in without saying a single word, and he kissed me.

I kissed him back.

After some time, he pulled away; we were both out of breath. I smiled at him, but he didn't return the smile. He just kept looking at me and breathing heavily. I reached my hand out to grab his, but he quickly placed his arms to his side. I didn't understand. My heart kept pounding.

"Jeffery?" I whispered, unsure of his reaction.

But all he did was shake his head and sigh. He looked down at the ground, and the smile that usually sat peacefully on his face was nowhere to be seen. It almost looked like he was going to cry.

"Jeffery," I said again, this time more like a statement than a question.

He raised his eyes to look at me, and we both just stood there. Then he lifted his hands to me, like a sign of surrender, and without a word quietly took a few steps back. He then turned and walked away.

"Jeffery!" I cried out, desperately.

I might have been imagining things, but I thought I heard him say, "I'm sorry," and then he was gone.

Chapter 9

I was angry. My heart was broken. I didn't understand what had just happened. And mostly I just wanted to be back in Jeffery's presence – kissing or no kissing; it didn't matter. Ok, well maybe I would have preferred the "kissing" to the "no kissing." But mostly, I just missed him. I thought he would come and apologize; tell me he was overwhelmed with emotion, something romantic like that. But it never happened. I never saw him in the hallway. I never got a phone call or a message. He was simply gone.

Ironically, the sunshine that had been greeting me every morning for weeks turned into dark clouds. I didn't want to face the days, and I certainly didn't want to turn on the radio and hear any love songs. I was disgusted by the honeymooners who were roaming the beaches each night, and I didn't know whether to feel hurt because I was missing Jeffery, or angry because he left me in such an abrupt way. I couldn't talk to anyone about it since I hadn't made that many friends, and obviously I wasn't going to mention it to my parents. The last thing I needed was for them to flip out over their daughter kissing some older man. So I was alone.

Well, not entirely. There was Noa. He had been the only other constant in my life since moving to Hawai'i, and though we hadn't really talked about deep and personal issues before, I felt like he was the one guy on the island who had my back. Some friends are like that. You don't have to see them that often, and they don't even need to know you that well. But they're steadfast, and in the end, they are what real friends are all about.

So after about a week of moping around my condo, I pulled myself together and went down to the Koi Café.

"Waaaaaaay long time, no see!," Noa sarcastically said to me when I sat down in my usual corner.

"Yeah, I know," I replied with a less than enthusiastic tone and a slightly bitter look on my face.

"Whoa, sista," he said, as he put down the coffee pot and slid in next to me along the booth.

I didn't have to say anything more. He threw his arm around me and gave me a squeeze. That's all it took before the smile-of-surrender came to my face and tears starting releasing themselves.

Noa was great. He was more than great – he was amazing. He listened to me for over an hour. And I mean really listened, not that fake type of listening most people do. He shut the whole world out and was completely tuned into what I was telling him. His cousin, Jay, took care of the customers; he, too, could tell I needed a friend. Island boys truly are special.

Noa sympathized with me, and he soon had me laughing at some of the more humorous moments of my tale – like spilling tea in Jeffery's living room. He also tried to help me see all of it from a different viewpoint. So often we think our perspective is the only one there is. But that's never the case. Jeffery obviously had his reasons for backing away. Noa said he could clearly tell Jeffery cared deeply for me, but that for whatever reason he needed to "go catch a wave." That was Noa's gentle way of telling me Jeffery was gone.

"Da ocean does dat to us sometimes, sista," he said.

"What? What are you talking about?" I replied.

"Da ocean – some days it brings us beautiful treasures. You ever find a *conch* shell on da beach? Das from da ocean. And it's da same ocean dat make me wipe out on my board and hit my head on da rocks. Some days da waves are gentle, some days dey rough. But the ocean ain't goin' nowhere. It still gonna sing you to sleep every night, no madda you upset with it or lov'n it. Da ocean is da ocean. You can't change it. Better to just ride da waves and trust everything gonna be alright."

That shut me up. I still wasn't happy, but I didn't feel like complaining anymore right then, either. Noa took something off the window ledge opposite my table, and then walked back over my way. With his bleached t-shirt and white apron tied around his waist, he leaned down close to my face. Sheepishly, I hunched down a bit myself. Noa took my hand that had been tearing napkins earlier and was now in a fist, and he opened it. He placed a little white shell inside, kissed my cheek, and gave me a big smile. The corner of my lip raised a bit and I gave him a half smile in return. Then he picked up the coffee pot and started refilling cups.

Chapter 10

I had never been so happy to see the end of an academic term. Thankfully, the parting of ways between Jeffery and me happened just two weeks before I was scheduled to go back to the mainland for a brief vacation. It feels silly calling time away from Hawai'i a "vacation," but that's what it was, and I needed it desperately.

Mom and Dad were happy to have me home, but I could also feel a change between us. They treated me more like an adult, one who had her own life and didn't need to be bothered by needy parents. The funny thing was that I wanted to be hounded by them; I wanted them to care and smother me. A small part of me even wanted to tell them about Jeffery. But I couldn't. It was just too awkward, and emotionally I couldn't handle any more drama. So I did the next best thing; I went to see Auntie Mele.

If Mom and Dad were happy to have me home, Auntie was thrilled. She beamed when she saw me standing at her door holding a bag of her favorite goodies from "home," and she threw her arms around me so tightly that it almost hurt.

"Let me look at you!" she said with a huge beaming smile. How could you not love her?

During the months I had been away, I was actually pretty good about writing to Auntie on a weekly basis, and I even sent her a couple care packages after receiving one from her. She had flown Washington apples and Starbucks coffee across the ocean just so I wouldn't forget where I came from. I didn't have the heart to tell her I could have easily picked them up at the supermarket near the condo. But for some reason, I swear those Golden Delicious apples tasted better than the ones at the store. When I told Auntie that, she smiled.

"Of course they did," she said. "That's because I packed loved all around each of those apples in the box before I sent them." Of course.

Even though I was doing my best to put on a happy face, Auntie knew me well enough to know something was troubling my heart. She patiently waited for me to finish giving her updates about school and Noa before she tilted her head in that knowing way of hers. She gave me "the look."

"So… what's his name?" she asked.

There was no use in denying it, but I just wasn't ready to say it out loud yet; not with her, not with anyone on the mainland. So I just sat there biting the inside of my cheek. My eyes moved from hers to the coffee table, back to her, and back to the table.

She sat back, took in a big breath and squinted her eyes.

"I see," she said, followed by a long exhale. "He's a teacher."

No, he wasn't my teacher, and I told her as much. He didn't work at the college or any school at all.

"Oh yes," she said very confidently, "he is most certainly a teacher. You've got it written all over your face."

I was puzzled why she kept insisting that Jeffery was something that I clearly knew he wasn't.

"No, Auntie, you really must be mistaken," I tried to nicely tell her. "He's not an instructor."

"Maybe not," she said, "but he is most definitely in your life *for a reason*."

Auntie Mele got up from out of her arm chair, walked a few steps, and sat down next to me on the sofa. She turned her body towards me and put her face directly in front of mine. I knew there was no getting around what she was about to say. The white crocheted doily that always sat on the arm of the sofa fell to the floor, but I didn't bother to pick it up. My eyes were glued to Auntie's.

"You don't have to tell me anything, my dear. I can see your heart on your sleeve. You love him, and he broke your heart. He's probably a good man; but he just couldn't be the man you wanted him to be. Sweetheart, there are only three types of people in this world: the ones who come into our lives for a reason, the ones who stay for a whole season, and those who are with us for a lifetime.

"The last group is easy to recognize; they are usually our family members and dearest friends. They can even be people from the supermarket you see every day, or the doctor who's been with your family for years.

"The people who walk with us for a season are in our lives for a particular section of time. Perhaps they are childhood friends who we've grown up with, or people that we date for years but never marry. They can even be second marriages.

"But it's the folks who enter our lives for a reason that are our most distinguished guests; they are our teachers. Sometimes they are vibrant characters who show us how to embrace life and live less seriously. Other times they can be people we despise, or people who shake us at our core. Ultimately those folks end up teaching us how *not* to be. But sometimes, as difficult as it sounds, the people who have the most to teach us are the ones we deeply care for, and for whatever reason, don't stay very long. They teach us about the most important things in life – about love and forgiveness, and about ourselves – and then they move on. No one ever said the lessons would be easy. But I can promise you this, dear one: the teacher will never show up if the student isn't ready to learn."

And with that, she wrapped one arm around me and placed her other hand on top of mine. I still hadn't said much, but I knew the tears on my cheeks were saying enough.

After some time, I wiped my face and picked up the doily from the floor. I told Auntie the whole story – from the day Jeffery and I met over my dropped groceries to the last time I saw him in the hallway. I hadn't realized until that moment that he and I had met and parted in pretty much the same place. Auntie said she didn't know if I'd hear from him again, and she told me not to get my hopes up.

"Girls always tend to do that," she said. "They wait, and they wait, and they wait. But many times, they are simply left waiting. It's ok to hope and to keep on loving from a distance, but don't forget to *live*. So much of life ends up passing you by if you just sit around waiting. And even though I'm a romantic, I am here to tell you, sweetheart, no one is worth wasting your life for. No one.

"Go back to the island, my sweet girl. Open your arms wide and welcome what gifts it has in store for you. There are still treasures to be found, and adventures to be had. There are flowers to be strung, and dances to be learned. But mostly, there is love to be shared; go and find it. It's waiting for you."

As soon as she was finished, she stood up and started heading towards the kitchen. She told me it was time for me to go home because she had things to do. She had *never* kicked me out of her house before, and I knew she wasn't really doing it this time, either. But I graciously got my things together and walked to the door. Just as I was about to turn the handle, I swung my head around.

"Are you really not at all bothered by the fact that Jeffery was old enough to be my dad?" Auntie just laughed as she stepped out into the hallway.

"Oh honey, love always comes in the package we least expect."

With that, she wiped her hands on the checkered dish towel around her waist and walked back into the kitchen.

Chapter 11

That evening I sat down and made a list. I had originally planned for it to be a list of pros and cons; all the reasons why it was good to have Jeffery in my life versus all the reasons why I was glad to see him go. But who was I trying to fool? The list ended up being a culmination of Jeffery's qualities, along with the ways in which he had changed my life.

I first thought about his character. I honestly couldn't think of a kinder man, and I had a hard time trying to picture him angry. I had never seen him upset, and I gathered it rarely happened, if ever. He went out of his way to make others comfortable, whether that meant offering the better seat or lightening an awkward situation. He was gentle and sensual, which I experienced firsthand in the way he led me by the small of my back when exiting a room. He was carful with his words – never wanting to offend or talk over anyone, though he was more well read than most and probably had more letters after his name than I'd ever dream of having. And, he listened. He never interrupted when I spoke, but rather took in every word I said. He treated me like an equal, and never once made me feel like a child.

Jeffery challenged my way of thinking and he pushed me, knowing that I would rise to the higher bar he set. He helped broaden my view of the world and of my place in it. But mostly, he helped me think about my own life in a new way. He clearly wanted the best for me, and he wanted me to find all that life had waiting.

"There are little gifts along the path with your name on them," he had said.

He was light hearted and laughed easily, and whenever I was around him the whole world seemed to quiet down. He made me feel special. He made me feel beautiful. He made me feel like a woman.

The only thing I could write in the other column was his age.

Before I'd met Jeffery, I'd had crushes on several guys, and I even dated a few. They were usually star athletes, beautifully built with perfect hair, and they had that certain sex appeal that made girls write their names over and over again during AP History class. Some of them could afford taking girls to the best restaurants, and others were famous for having flowers delivered to afternoon classes. One boyfriend sang in a band and usually dedicated his first song of the night to me; he also drove a convertible. Jeffery didn't have any of those things. But he had my heart.

Why was it that a man twice my age and who was losing his hair was able to touch me in a place so far inside of myself that I had never even known it existed? And why was he here one minute and then simply gone the next?

"Because he was here to teach you about love," I could hear Auntie saying in my head.

Jeffery's kindness far outweighed other men's charms and good looks. His gentleness and respect towards women, and the way in which he empowered me to always strive for my ideals in life, to not settle for less than what I truly wanted and deserved, and to believe – most especially when others thought I was being unrealistic or crazy – those were the gifts he had given me, and they were far sexier than sculpted muscles or a fast car.

Jeffery had become the standard by which I would judge all future men. He showed me what love should really look like, and he ignited something within me that wanted to believe in the dream. Not only did I believe in it, but I was determined to find it.

In leaving me the way he did, Jeffery also taught me how to love from a distance. Just because he walked away didn't mean that I had to. There was no rule saying I had to stop feeling the way I did. Instead, I wanted to believe that somewhere in his heart he would always feel my care for him, even if we were apart.

Jeffery and I had never talked about God, but we had discussed the stars. We both liked sitting on the sand at night, looking up at all the diamonds in the sky. It reminded me of people holding candles during the Christmas Eve candlelight service. Everyone lights candles for their own reasons – some big, some small – but to Heaven they must all look the same; a prayer is a prayer, no matter how significant or mundane. I had to trust that those sparkling gems were watching over us now, and that no matter where we were in the world, Orion would always find a way to hold us together.

Jeffery taught me how to love and how to be loved, and then he stepped aside, making room for the rest of my life to begin.

Chapter 12

Noa was waiting for me when I walked into the Café on my first morning back on O'ahu. Big smile, bleach-white shirt, and papaya with lime on a little plastic plate.

"*Aloha*, sista!" he said with sunshine bursting from his words. I admit, it was good to be back.

I wasn't really sure what I was going to do with myself now that I was no longer hanging out with Jeffery. Aside from school, evenings with

Jeffery had become a common occurrence. But now it was time to start a new chapter, as Auntie had explained, and I didn't have the foggiest clue where to begin. Thankfully, I didn't have to wait long to figure it out.

"You got plans tonight, sis?" asked Noa, while setting down a plate of fried eggs and wheat toast for the customer seated next to me.

"What do you think?" I said with a slight smile. "Of course I don't."

"Well, you do now," Noa shouted for the whole place to hear. "Me and da boys are heading to Lanikai tonight to hang out. You should come."

What did I have to lose? Honestly, it sounded great. He told me he'd pick me up at 7:30 in front of the condo, and to bring a zip-up jacket in case the breeze picked up. He didn't want me to be cold.

As usual, I was ready early, but decided to just sit on the curb outside the building until the boys arrived. I didn't see any reason in going back up twelve floors to just come down them again in a few minutes. I also didn't want to run into Jeffery.

The sun was beginning to set, and it felt like time stood still for a brief moment. Everything was calm and my worries were put on pause. The red, pink, and orange colors of the sunset looked like those you would find in a fruit bowl, and the whole sky was lit up like it was on fire. It was magnificent, like a painting hovering over the island, and I just couldn't help feeling that something, or someone, was telling me everything would be all right.

About the moment I was getting a little too sentimental looking off into the distance, Noa and the boys drove up in a broken down forest green pick-up. Jay, Noa's cousin from the Café, was driving, and the back end was filled with some of their surfer friends. I'd seen most of them a time or two when I was having breakfast, but we'd never spoken. I felt a bit awkward joining them, seeing as how I was the only girl. But all of that washed away the minute the truck stopped.

"Eh, sista!" one of them shouted at me.

"Jump on in, girl!" another yelled.

All of them had big warm smiles on their faces as they waved me over, and Noa just laughed.

"You's in good hands now, lil sis," he said. "Buckle in, it's gonna be a crazy ride."

Noa wasn't kidding. The ride through the *Pali*, though beautiful, was insane. Jay drove like a mad man in between the lush green mountains, and the truck felt like it was a horse taking its last run. The boys in the back just laughed and hollered, and before long I was shouting along with them. My grief had stayed home for the night, and with the wind in my face, I felt alive.

Jay parked the truck in someone's driveway – I assumed he must have known them – and we all piled out. We walked along the side of the house, taking a short path that lead to the beach. A small fire was burning when we reached the sand; three other surfers had gotten there before us and had already cracked open a six pack of beer and a bag of chips. They'd brought a cooler full of hot dogs and drinks, and for a reason I couldn't understand, they had a few tins of Spam. I later learned that Hawaiian boys love the stuff.

One of the guys was playing his version of Bob Marley's "One Love" on his guitar, while the other two sang along. We could hear their music and laughter even before we saw them. The boys from the truck joined in as we reached the fire, but I was too shy to just burst into song. I knew the words, but I didn't want to embarrass myself. I never liked karaoke, even though it was all the rage, and I was scared as heck to sing in public. Only the inside of my shower knew what my singing voice sounded like. The guys didn't seem to care that I wasn't signing, and instead handed me a beer and welcomed me into their circle. My face held a smile the whole night.

Noa quickly introduced me to everyone when we first sat down, but I couldn't have told you their names five minutes later. I'm terrible at remembering such things. All I knew was that these guys were warm and friendly, and they clearly enjoyed one another's company. They sang, drank, roasted hotdogs, and savored their beloved Spam.

As usual, the main topic of conversation in between reggae songs was surfing. I began to understand that each wave truly held significance for them, and I could see they lived in the moment when they were out on their boards. They couldn't worry about past waves or wipe outs, nor could they fantasize about what might be coming down the pike. They had to focus in on the wave at hand. If they didn't, they would miss their opportunity for something spectacular, or they might even get hurt. The rush they got from surfing put them on a constant high, even when they weren't on the water, and their relationship with the sea was one of awe, respect and kinship. There was a natural ebb and flow to the way these surfers lived their lives, and just like the song, they trusted that "every little thing was gonna be all right." You gotta love Bob Marley.

The evening began to draw to a close, and I was sad to see it end. Noa had been right about several things; I'd had a great time, and the wind had definitely picked up. Who would have known I would get cold in Hawai'i? It was a lucky thing that I'd brought a jacket. I still hadn't joined in with the singing, but I had used the cooler as a drum, and I even humored Eddie by tasting a piece of his toasted Spam. (Honestly, I still couldn't see the attraction.) All in all, it had been a great night. When the guys dropped me off at the condo, they told me to come out with them again sometime. I agreed and told them I'd love to. The dark-green truck pulled out of the parking lot, and I felt immense gratitude; how lucky I was to have such great friends – ones I had just met. My heart was light, and I knew I would sleep well that night. I looked up at the stars, and at that very moment one of those little diamonds shot across the sky. I burst out laughing.

"I think God just winked at me," I said to no one in particular. Then, as if right on cue, a second star went flying by.

Chapter 13

The funny thing about beginning new chapters in life is that you really do move forward. Before the new phase begins, there's always a transitional period. Sometimes it's short; sometimes it's long. But eventually, and usually without even realizing it, you find yourself standing on a new page.

It's a beautiful feeling; walking along the crisp white paper before any words have been written. The whole world is out there for you to grab, and you haven't even yet started dipping your fountain pen in black ink.

The bottom line is that life gives us opportunities to start again.

We take with us all that has been a part of our journey up to that point; experiences, lessons, joys, sorrows. Each of them decorates our story. Some characters will venture with us from one chapter to the next. Others will simply make special guest appearances for a select amount of time; one is not better than the other. (This is exactly what Auntie Mele was trying to tell me.)

Often times the people who leave the strongest impact are the ones who visit us for brief moments, while the folks we see every day sometimes seem like strangers. Life is ironic that way.

It can be very scary trying to take the next step. Yet when the new page is sitting there, staring us in the face, it's our job to grab it with all our might. Perhaps we've come from a celebration in the past, or maybe we've just barely survived. Either way, like a lively parade, life moves on in a new direction. It's always calling our name, asking us to follow and join. We really shouldn't miss the show.

Noa shared with me another way of thinking about this. He said that the ocean was like life – beautiful, vast, full of hidden details below the surface, and choppy. Our responsibility was to stay as glued to our boards as possible. There would be days when the waves were "sweet" and we could glide all the way into shore. Other days would be tragic, maybe even bloody. Falling off was part of the growing process. But drowning wasn't an option. We had to use our *mana*, our strength, to come up out of the waves, shake the water from our face, and paddle hard – real hard – until we made it back. If a board broke in two, it wasn't the end of the world.

"Why you think there's so many board shops out dere, sista?" he would ask and then laugh.

I had to admit it made a lot of sense, and it also looked like I was about to learn to surf.

So there I was, standing on a brand new piece of paper, ready to write my next chapter. I tried not to look back. I tried not to think too far ahead. Instead, I took a deep breath, looked out at the ocean, and I jumped.

I was scared as hell, but I did it anyway.

PART III

Chapter 14

Time doesn't heal all wounds, but it does lessen the sting. We all end up acquiring scars from life that we wear like badges; often times pinned on the heart instead of the skin. They represent moments of challenge, strength, beauty and growth. They are a part of us, but they are not *who* we are. We should never be fooled into thinking they define our lives, because they don't. Sadly, some of us seem to fall into this trap. The continual picking of a scab only allows the wound to relive itself over and over again.

But if we nurture it and learn from its pain, we will become wiser and more compassionate. Inevitably, our wounds and their meanings end up having something to do with the paths our lives ultimately travel on.

A few months had gone by since returning to the islands, and I actually felt as if I had grown up a lot in that short period of time. Loss does that to us, I suppose. Innocence and invincibility seem to fly out the window, along with the dreams that had always seemed so realistic.

There were times when I got depressed. I would feel sorry for myself and uncertain about why life had gone the way it had. But thankfully those moments were brief. Mostly, I just walked into each day with no expectations; partly because I wanted to be surprised, but mainly because I didn't want to be disappointed. I suppose I was just protecting myself.

"When life cuts away branches from the tree, it makes room for new ones. It also makes the tree stronger," Auntie Mele had explained long ago. This was the way she described her life after her husband died.

"We must prune back in winter if we want to bloom in spring," she had said. As always, she was right.

During those days, I felt a new kind of strength come into me. It could have been *mana*, but I think it was probably just maturity. Eventually, the dreams I had tossed out the window started to come back again, and I began picking up the pieces and moving onward.

On the weekends, I hung out with Noa and his friends more regularly. Believe it or not, I even began singing along to a few reggae tunes on the beach. The guys didn't make a big deal of it. They just smiled at me and nodded their heads. It was their way of being supportive. I hadn't shared with any of them about what had been taking place in my personal life, but assumed Noa might have. They never asked any questions, and yet they all seemed to be "in the know." They were also protective of me; it was sweet, and I really treasured becoming part of their group.

I put my energies back into my studies, and watched my grades pick up like they had been at the beginning of the year. Tuesday and Thursday nights I stayed late on campus to volunteer with a tutoring group; I was helping local adults learn to read. It was one of the most rewarding things I had ever done. The only drawback was that it meant I was on campus all day and didn't leave until late at night. By the time I finished up with my last client, I was usually drained and sometimes even falling asleep on the bus ride home. The summer heat didn't help matters much, either.

One evening after tutoring, I got on the bus and instantly leaned my head against the glass window. The top part of the window had been lowered so the breeze could blow through, but there was still a small section of glass I could sleep against. The bus sat parked for about ten minutes as it waited to collect any last minute stragglers. There were a couple overhead fans doing their best, but most of us were still uncomfortably hot. My eyes were heavy, and my lids only slightly open. That's when I first saw her.

She was looking right at me. My eyes widened a bit, and I lifted up my head. At that moment I wasn't exactly sure if she was a girl or a boy. I guess the politically correct term would have been "androgynous." It didn't seem to matter; all I knew was that she'd gotten my attention. She kept looking right at me, which weirded me out but also filled me with some sort of strange excitement at the same time. I guess you could say I was mesmerized.

I don't know what it was about her, exactly; she was far from beautiful or handsome. Instead, she was radiating nonconformity, uniqueness, and a tad bit of what some might even consider sexy. She was pierced, tattooed, and highlighted. I'd even go so far as saying she was cute; she literally had a miniature Hello Kitty hanging from her Goth backpack. I just kept staring.

"Are you the one?" she asked.

"Excuse me?" I replied, unsure of whether she was talking to me.

"Yeah man, you're Eddie's friend, right?" she responded.

She shoved her hands into her pockets and shrugged her shoulders upwards. It was like she was nervous about something. Then she slipped out a slight giggle and her eyes twinkled. I couldn't help but to smile in return.

"Yeah, um... I guess so," I replied

I didn't know what else to say. I was taken aback; almost giddy. Maybe I actually was. What was it about this girl?

"Thought so," she said as she nodded her head with a very satisfied look.

I still had no clue who she was. I wanted to at least ask her name, but she started to pass me and walk down the aisle towards the back of the bus. Just when I thought I lost my chance, she leaned in towards me and whispered.

"I'm Kekoa. Eddie told me I'd probably see you here."

My face looked straight ahead and all the little hairs on my arms began to rise. Just the feel of her breath near my ear made me tingle. I was frozen; not cold, just stunned. I wasn't even breathing. Then somehow I managed to turn my head ever so slightly to face her. There she was, staring at me. Her eyes were beautiful and deep. They were black, just like her short hair and chipped nail polish. But they were also surprisingly gentle. After a moment she giggled, and then walked on. My eyes dropped to the floor, and I looked down at my orange shoes that matched my dress. There was a smile all across my face. I sat like that for a minute or so, and then my hand moved to my lips.

"Kekoa," I whispered out loud, hidden behind my fingers.

The entire ride home I kept my eyes looking forward. When the bus reached the stop near the condo, I gathered my bag and tried to nonchalantly glance behind me. Most people had already gotten off by that point, so she was easy to spot. Kekoa had tucked herself into the back right-hand corner. She looked at me when I stood up, so I gave a little smile and a wave. She returned them with a slight upwards nod.

"Later, man" she called out.

"Yeah, ok," I replied. Then I got off the bus, and looked up; the moon was full and shining bright, and I smiled all the way home.

Chapter 15

My daily breakfast papaya seemed a bit tangier than usual the next morning. Maybe it was the special way Noa squeezed the lime over top, but I rather doubt it. I had a new color floating around in my head – a shade of black I had never seen before. It had a shine to it, a brightness, like the sun was reflecting off of it; *a light in the darkness*. As cliché as it sounded, that's exactly what I kept seeing in my mind, and I was fascinated.

I hadn't been sitting on the bar stool long when Eddie came strolling into the Café. His shorts were still damp from his morning surf, and his hair was all over the place. He rolled up onto the stool next to me and flashed that infamous charming smile of his. I had just shoved some fruit into my mouth, and I thought it would be rude if I tried to speak, so I didn't say hello.

"Hey, No – can I get a cup of joe from ya, brah?" he hollered out at Noa.

"Sure thing, brudda," Noa called back from the swinging doors that lead to the kitchen.

Eddie turned his attention back towards me and flashed me another great smile while he rested his folded hands and elbows on the counter.

"So, little sis, I understand you met my girl last night," he said with a twinkle in his eye.

I didn't know what to say, and so I didn't say anything. He kept looking at me, smiling, like there was a secret hidden just behind his lips. However, I clearly didn't know what it was. And then it dawned on me: Kekoa. How in the world did he know about that? I just met her for a brief moment the night before (and I had been looking quite run down, I might add.) We hadn't really talked at all, and I hadn't even given her my name. Apparently such things didn't matter if she'd already told Eddie. Wow! News travels fast in Hawai'i.

"Are you referring to Kekoa," I asked shyly.

"Yep, that's her," he replied as Noa handed him a cup of hot coffee. "Thanks, brah."

Noa wink at me and nodded at Eddie in return.

"I'm sorry, Eddie. I didn't know she was your girlfriend. And to tell you the truth, we didn't really have a chance to talk much," I said. "You know, being on the bus and all."

I know I was being juvenile. Of course we *could* have talked on the bus, but I knew I hadn't been in a place where I could have carried on much of a conversation. I had been overwhelmed by her in those fleeting moments that took place between us, and I could tell Eddie knew it, too.

"Oh sure, right," he said as he dropped some sugar cubes into his cup. He clearly didn't believe what either of us was saying. "Besides, what are you sorry about? For the record, she's not my girlfriend."

"Oh?" replied. "But I thought you said…"

"She's my *girl*, yeah," confirmed Eddie. "You know, we hang out, we surf together, that sort of thing. But beyond that, I'm not her type."

"Oh," I replied, trying to make sense of all this.

"Let's just say Kekoa is probably more interested in you than she is in me," he said with a constant smile on his face, followed by a big sip of what had become very sweet coffee. "She's into girls, if you couldn't already tell. And little sis, you left quite an impression on her." Then he chuckled.

I didn't say anything. I didn't know how I was supposed to respond. Eddie looked back over at me and started to laugh.

"Don't look so serious. It's all cool," he said. "Listen, I gotta run. Sorry I can't stay and chat. We'll catch up later. See ya around."

"Yeah, ok," I managed to get out.

"Later, No," he yelled towards the kitchen, and then he downed the last of his coffee. Noa stuck his arm out the door and waved. Eddie jumped down from the stool, patted me on the shoulder, and then walked off, leaving me there at the counter to process by myself. I hadn't at all seen any of *that* coming.

After the customer rush slowed down, Noa came over to my counter and took a brief break from refilling coffee cups.

"You doin' ok, sis?" he asked. "You seem like you got a lot on your mind. Something new happen with Jefferey?"

Jeffery! Oh gosh, I hadn't even thought about him all day. This new preoccupation of mine had absolutely nothing to do with him, except for the fact that it had taken over my concentration the same way the memory of Jeffery's scent once did.

"No, no. Nothing like that," I told him. "Eddie and I were just talking about someone we knew, that's all."

"Kekoa," he said. "So I've heard. I understand you met her last night on da bus."

Oh my goodness! Did the whole island know? The difference between Eddie and Noa's reactions was that Noa didn't seem quite as excited about my new acquaintance. In all fairness, I couldn't even call her that. A few moments of formalities in the aisle of a bus didn't actually constitute friendship.

So if that was true, then why were so many of us talking about it?

"Does anything *not* get talked about on this island?" I asked as I shook my head.

"You're right, gossip is catchin' 'round these parts, but don't worry," said Noa. "Da boys and I were surfing with Kekoa dis mornin', and that's when she told us about your chance encounter last night. I guess Eddie had given her da heads up that you might be dere."

"Do you guys surf with her often," I asked.

"From time to time," he said. "She comes and goes for long stretches. I haven't really gotten too friendly with her, but Eddie might be able to tell you more about her. Da two of dem seem pretty close."

I finished off the last of my fruit as Noa picked up the coffee pot, making the rounds once again. I pulled a few dollars out of my wallet and set them down on the counter. The conversation from a few minutes before kept playing in my head. It seemed that Eddie was the person I needed to talk with if I was going to get any answers about the new girl who just walked into my life. With that thought in hand, I grabbed my flee market bag and walked back out into the morning sun.

Chapter 16

So… Kekoa's gay, a voice kept saying in my head. As far as I knew, I had never had a gay friend before, at least not someone I was close to. I wasn't really sure how to feel about this. Was I supposed to have some kind of reaction to the news, like disgust or fear, or did it even matter at all? I was at a loss.

But what was truly tugging at me was the way I had reacted when I first saw her on the bus. There was nothing dark or scary about our meeting, aside from her Goth wear, and instead I felt energized by it.

In that brief moment, it was like she lit a candle inside me I didn't even know I held. What did that say about me?

I wasn't ready to delve too deeply into these questions, but they never left my mind either. No matter how I tried to distract myself, they were still hovering close by. The strangest part about it was that even though I didn't understand these thoughts, I was fascinated by them, the same way I was fascinated with her.

Gay – a word that had sparked so much debate, controversy, and hatred, as well as celebration, pride, and joy over the years. My parents had never talked to me about it, aside from the fact that my mother always mentioned wanting me to marry a "nice young man" to raise a family with. Neither of them was very religious, and the church we attended on Christmas Eve never seemed to make a statement one way or another to its annual guests. I was fortunate to grow up in Seattle, a fairly diverse and liberal city, but we also had our fair share of conservative folks in the Pacific Northwest, too.

A couple times a month the nearby college campus unfortunately had to deal with homophobic evangelicals who whole-heartedly believed they were doing God's will by shouting hateful language at gay students. Their gigantic signs with equally hurtful messages could be seen from across campus, and sadly the college couldn't do anything about them since it was public property. Such actions always made me angry for the people it hurt and sad for the faith based groups who were embarrassed. It's extremely scary to see what some people will do in God's name. I imagine He must be shaking His head.

I thought about a girl I went to high school with who turned out to be gay. Back then I didn't know how to react to that revelation, either. I worried about what she might have been thinking when we were changing in the locker room for P.E. I was curious if her Homecoming date had just been a ruse to fool everyone. I even went so far as imagining her kissing another girl. But then I stopped being ridiculous. I figured she was no different the day before when I hadn't known about her orientation, and she had most definitely been gay a lot longer than one day. I'd never had a problem with her in the past, so why should I now? Surprisingly, after a couple weeks, I seemed to have forgotten about it. P.E. didn't change any or feel any less comfortable; when we were put together in the same group for science lab, she didn't give me any strange glances or make any moves; and she was really helpful when I was having trouble with my calculus problems during midterms. My fears and worries had been unfair stereotypes that obviously proved themselves false. So if that hadn't been a big deal, then finding out Kekoa was gay shouldn't have been either.

I had agreed to meet the guys the following evening. They were having another one of their beach barbeques, complete with singing and Spam. I rode with Noa and another friend, which meant we arrived a little later than the others; Noa had to tidy up the Café before we could leave. With a couple bags of lime flavored chips in hand, we flew up the road through the Pali as quickly as we could. The sun had already dipped below the horizon when our feet finally touched the sand, but the fire was blazing and the singing was loud. We had no trouble finding them.

"First things first," Eddie said as we arrive on the scene. "Coke or beer?" I chose Coke. He pulled one out from the ice cooler and handed it to me.

"Hot dog or Spam?" he asked next with a mischievous smile on his lips. He knew I wasn't really into his favorite "tin of goodness," as he liked to refer to it.

"I think I'm going to have to opt for a hot dog this time," I answered.

"Wise choice," I heard someone say from the opposite side of the fire. I couldn't make out the face because the flames had gotten really high, and the voice was sitting on the sand. I squinted my eyes, trying to see through them, but no luck. Then for only a brief moment the orange tongue of the fire moved aside and I saw her. It was Kekoa.

"Oh, hi!" I said, surprised to see her. "I didn't know you were going to be here." I moved myself around the fire and sat down next to her.

"Yeah, man," she said, moving over a bit to make some room for me. "Eddie told me everyone was coming out tonight, so I thought 'why not?'"

"Sounds good," I said, sounding stupid because I didn't know what else to say. My heart was beating really quickly; I had been caught off guard when I saw her just then. It was a combination of surprise and excitement.

And then I heard the little voice in my head again: *She's gay,* my mind reminded me, *and you're not. Remember Jeffery?* I knew those two things were true, and I couldn't explain why, but I also knew I wanted to be friends with her. *Don't worry about it*, I snapped back in return. It was quiet the rest of the evening.

Time flew by that night. I honestly don't remember much other that talking with Kekoa, or K, as she liked to be called. We sat by the fire the whole time as the boys roasted up the goods and kept bottles flowing through our hands all evening. K seemed to be going through one bottle of beer after another. I was surprised. She didn't seem drunk, though she should have been given her very tall but thin frame. Plus, she hardly ate anything.

K giggled constantly. She laughed at her own stories, and she seemed to listen intently to mine, though I hardly ever saw her look me in the eye. Mostly we kept the conversation on the surface, lightly dipping into other subjects as they came up. I told her how I'd come to O'ahu, and I found out she'd been born there. She was an only child, like me, and her parents were never around; business deals and travel were more important to them. Her relatives were scattered throughout several of the islands, so she island-hopped quite often. She invited me to go with her if I wanted to sometime. I told her I would keep it in mind.

She had been taking college classes as a way to stay busy. Music had always been her passion, but

K's parents wanted her to do more than just play guitar. Her band performed most Fridays and Saturdays, and she invited me to come hear them the following weekend. We got onto talking about how I met Noa and the boys, and she wanted to know whether I had ever been out on the waves with them. I asked her how long she'd been surfing, and like most of the guys, she'd been in the water from the time she could float.

"Weren't you scared of sharks," I asked, holding my knees up to my chest in a protective gesture.

"Nah man, Mano's always got my back out there." She then proceeded to tell me all about her shark god.

It was the first time I had heard someone talk about one of the Hawaiian gods in such a personal way. Usually explanations were more mythical, but K was serious. Mano was very real to her, and her admiration for him was sincere. She trusted him to protect her when she was in the water, but even more importantly, she valued the sense of friendship she believed she had with him. I'm not one to question another's beliefs, but I was having a hard time understanding all that she was saying. Could she really be telling me that the most feared creature in the sea was her confidant? Yes, she was. As the night went on and she continued to explain, I began to understand that the spirit of this big fish was her totem, her personal God, but mostly, it was her friend.

Eddie left us alone throughout the night. He didn't even bother me with any toasted Spam offers. But a couple times I caught his eye through the smoke and flames. He was watching us, and each time he had a knowing smile across his face. "What?!" I wanted to ask him. But secretly I knew the answer; I was probably glowing.

Talking with Kekoa was like jumping into a cool lake on a hot summer's day. She awakened all my senses and made me feel alive. I don't know how she did it exactly, but she did. She was refreshing. She swore unapologetically, laughed easily, and not once did I notice her without a beer bottle or lit cigarette in her hand. She held her alcohol well up until the end of the night, and even then she still stayed calm. Where others might get loud after so much drinking, she just mellowed out. I made a mention of it to her, and she said the beer made her relax. She hadn't seemed stressed out the two times I'd been around her, but perhaps there was still a lot we had to learn about the other. Then as abruptly as she'd shown up, she stood and said she was leaving.

"Later, guys" she said as she flicked the last of her cigarette onto the sand.

"Catch ya on the waves, eh?" someone called out.

Kekoa nodded her head upwards, and with her hands shoved into her pockets headed to the water's edge. She walked away from our circle, but I could still make out the small glow of the cigarette she had just lit. The darkness enveloped her, and then she was gone.

Chapter 17

I overslept my alarm by two hours the next morning. That sort of thing never happened to me, and all I could do was laugh at myself when I realized what I had done. There was no point trying to make it to my one class of the day, so I stayed in bed and stared out the window of my room. At that time of the morning, the light reflecting off the water was so bright it looked like thousands of tiny pale yellow crystals were jumping the waves. Tourists were up and playing on the beach, a yoga class was stretching beneath the shade of a gigantic tree, and the fishermen were wrapping up their gear and heading home. The sea seemed happy.

Playing over the night before in my head, I knew *that* was the reason I had slept so late. I had been relaxed *and* invigorated at the same time; it must have drained me. The sea air always washed me into a calming state, but my evening with Kekoa was the true reason for my need to just be. My body was telling me something, and I needed to listen.

When I woke up just then, I felt the best I had in a long time. I was no longer weighed down by baggage from the past or concerns about the future. Instead, I was living in the moment. I was only thinking about *now*, and I wanted to live it as fully as I could. It was the first time I could relate to the boys and the way they approached the waves and their lives. I was going with the flow.

Since school was no longer on the agenda for the day, I grabbed the new book I had bought earlier in the week and headed to the Koi Café. On the way down the elevator, I made the decision to turn my typical morning coffee break into a longer session of reading and relaxation. I wanted to bask in the fabulous new-found sensation I was experiencing. As the lift reached the ground floor and the doors opened onto the lobby, my morning revere suddenly came to an abrupt halt. Jeffery was staying near the front doors.

The classic phrase "take my breath away" doesn't fully express the shock my system went through when I saw him. I had been so caught off guard that I not only forgot to breathe, but I failed to get out of the elevator. It wasn't until the doors closed and it started to rise up again that I realized I hadn't moved. My initial reaction was to return to my condo and just wait. Jeffery would have to move from the lobby eventually. But I knew that was silly. Where was my new-found courage? I hadn't done anything wrong, and we were both adults. There wasn't any reason why I couldn't just walk through the lobby and out onto the sidewalk.

My heart was racing, pounding out of my chest, and I just wanted to get the whole ordeal over with. So much for releasing all my past drama; I guess there's an ebb and flow to learning how to live in the moment. I pushed the button for the lobby a second time and braced myself for what I knew would be waiting for me once the doors opened. To my surprise, he wasn't there. I let out the huge breath I had been holding high in my chest and looked around very discretely. There was no Jeffery to be found. I wish I could honestly say I was relieved, but that would be lying. Part of me was disappointed. I'm not sure why, but I was.

Despite the shocking setback to the morning, I still wanted to spend some time at the Café with my new book. It was crammed with customers when I arrived, both inside and out. Noa had recently added plastic tables and chairs outside around the front entrance, which is where tourists loved to sit and work on their tans while sipping soy lattes and double cappuccinos. There was an open chair at the counter inside, so I grabbed it before my chance was taken away. I placed my book on the countertop and looked in my bag for a hair tie. The weather had heated up and the strands against my neck were annoying me. I wrapped it up in one sweep and tied it back.

"Eh…. glad to see you made it," a scratchy voice called out from directly behind me.

I quickly spun around. There was Kekoa, tucked into a back corner table. She was slouching in the white chair, with one foot up on the seat and the other dangling near the floor out of its flip-flop. The last moments of her cigarette were burning out and the ashtray next to her on the table was already half full. She was wearing sunglasses inside, and the black t-shirt of the day simply displayed a single swear word largely written in white. The whole visual was lacking in class.

"Oh hey….uh, hi," I managed to get out, still caught by surprise to see her sitting there.

This had already been a morning full of moments I hadn't expected, and I didn't know how many more I could take. Life is strange that way – some days you awake feeling like you can take on the world, and in a heartbeat everything changes. I suppose the opposite is also true; the worst of days can suddenly be turned right again with a single kindness, like when Jeffery helped my groceries out of the rain several months prior. I was starting to understand why the boys didn't take life so seriously. In all honesty, it was out of our control.

"Hey man," said K, "I thought you always came down here before heading to campus," clearly making it more out to be a question than a statement.

She sounded irritated that I hadn't shown up until now. What the heck? And besides, how did she know my schedule?

"Yeah, you're right. I usually do come down hear much earlier," I replied, a bit defensively. She didn't seem to be listening to me, though. "Just not this morning."

"I've been waitin' for ya, man. Didn't think you were gonna show," and she took the last drag of her cigarette before snuffing it out in the ashtray.

Now I was beginning to get irritated, myself. Neither of us had made any kind of plans to meet up with each other the next day, and I didn't like the fact that she was trying to make me feel guilty regarding something I knew nothing about. Without taking her glasses off, she cocked her head sideways and just stared. I started to get uncomfortable since neither of us was saying anything. Then her face broke into a huge smile, she reached for her pack of cigarettes, and began to giggle like a little girl.

"Ah man, it's all cool," she said as she slid another smoke out of the pack. "Just glad you didn't leave me hang'n, that's all."

Papaya and coffee arrived at the same moment she flicked her lighter. I never needed to order them anymore because Noa just knew.

"Morning, sunshine," he said as he placed my breakfast down on the table where K was sitting. "Glad to see you could join us."

K smiled at his comment, and Noa chuckled in my direction, but I wasn't laughing. I hadn't planned to sit with K, but since she had an open chair and my food was already there, I felt obligated. I wasn't really sure if I wanted to be with her right then. Kekoa was different that morning, not like she had been the night before. She was spacey, yet I could tell she wasn't hung over. Noa placed my cup of black coffee down on the table next to the fruit, and that's when I noticed he'd cut the lime into the shape of a heart. His sweet gesture made me smile.

"That's better," he said looking at me as he refilled K's coffee mug. "I'll let you two gals get down to your gabbin'," and he left us to continue with his refill rounds.

"I've never seen you here before," I said to her as I squeezed the lime over top of the fruit.

"Yeah man, it's been awhile since I've been to Noa's place," she replied while blowing smoke towards the ceiling.

So much for a relaxing morning to myself. I quickly finished off the breakfast and downed the last of my coffee when K asked me what I was up to for the afternoon. I didn't want to admit to her that I'd missed my class, and so instead I said I had some reading to do. I thought it would turn her off and send her away. But I was wrong.

She told me she knew of some "wicked" places where I could go hang out, places tourists didn't know about, and that she'd be happy to take me if I wanted. All of a sudden it was like her tough exterior shed away and this little girl came shining through. She was so excited. How could I say no?

I left some cash on the table and grabbed my bag from the chair. K had already picked up my book and the last of her cigarettes. Her truck parked out back was clearly in need of a wash, but it had an awesome sound system. She wasn't joking when she said music was her thing. The backpack I had seen her with on the bus was thrown onto the floor, and the miniature Hello Kitty smiled up at me as I sat down. I thought to myself, *what a combination!*

Tracy Chapman was on the radio singing about some fast car as K popped a cassette into the tape deck and cranked up the volume so we could *feel* it. I didn't recognize the singer at first, and when I asked her who it was, she proudly kept nodding her head as she shifted gears and told me it was her band. I was impressed. It turns out they'd even written their own music and lyrics, and I thought they sounded really good. She reminded me for the second time that they were going to be playing at a nearby pub in a few days, and once again invited me to come check them out. This time I said I'd seriously consider it.

I had no idea where Kekoa was taking us, but before long we were parked along the side of the road in the middle of what looked like nowhere. K jumped out of the truck and told me to grab my bag. I followed her down a trail that weaved in between several trees; *plumeria* blossoms in full bloom all around us, and their scent intoxicating. It took me back to the first *plumeria* flower I inhaled when Auntie Mele had them sent over to the mainland. They say scent is the strongest of the five senses. While walking on the path, I believed that very well could be true.

"What do you think?" K asked as we walked out onto a clearing I hadn't seen coming from inside the path of vegetation.

A huge gust of wind blew into my face as I walked past the last tree, pulling some of the hair out of my upsweep. I brushed back the strands that were covering my eyes and took in the view.

It was breathtaking. I assumed we were on the edge of the island, somewhere far from roads and people. Huge rocks laid themselves out like steps leading to the sea. There was no beach, however, just an overhang that must have been hundreds of feet above the surface of the water. Mist sprayed over the rocks when the waves crashed up against them, and the blue-green I had come to love so passionately stretched out as far as my eyes could see. K was right – they didn't tell you about this place in the guidebooks.

I was at a loss for words as I continued to look around me at the spectacular beauty that seemed to be untouched by man. There were no hotels, no buildings, no roads, no people. It's what I imagined Hawai'i must have been like long ago before the islands were discovered and taken over. I thought about Auntie Mele in that moment. She would have loved this.

"You ok?" K asked with a somewhat worried look on her face. I realized I hadn't said anything since leaving the cab of the truck.

"Oh, yes. Sorry, this is just so amazing," I replied. "You were right about knowing the places to come to."

We each smiled and walked down a ways on the rocks. K was like a professional, leaping from formation to formation. I wasn't as confident and needed to take a bit more time. A significantly large gap between two rocks forced me to pause before jumping, and K noticed my hesitation. She walked back over my way and reached out her hand for me to take. Without reading anything into it, I placed my hand into hers and held on tight. Her hand was soft and gentle. Once again, the outward mask she worked so hard to display every day didn't match the tenderness that kept slowly breaking through. Her nails, however, were still sporting chipped black paint. I had to chuckle.

"What's so funny?" she asked me as I jumped down onto the rock she was standing on.

"Your nails," I replied as I put my face close to hers and smiled. She laughed.

We walked on down a little further and found a leveled off bolder to plant ourselves on. K was kind enough to brush off the sand that had blown up on top of it before I sat down. She then hiked her knees up to her chest, wrapped her arms around them, and looked out toward the ocean. I took a little longer to get situated, trying to find a comfortable spot to sit on. I finally did and looked over at Kekoa. The look on her face told me she was already miles away. I knew not to disturb her, and so I didn't. Instead, I gathered my legs underneath me and looked out towards the horizon.

The breeze coming off the water was strong, blowing my hair away from my face and stinging my eyes slightly. I slowed down my breathing and listened to the rhythm of my breath. I could feel my heart beat – slow and steady – and imagined the waves and I were in rhythm with each other. I recalled the sound of the chanters in Auntie Mele's house and the way they used to make me feel. This was just like that: a universal language felt with the heart. In that moment, I was one with the ocean, the air, the ancients of old, and the girl sitting next to me.

We sat that way for a long time. Without realizing it, I closed my eyes and continued to breathe deeply. A few minutes passed, and then something gently awakened me out of my meditation; I saw K was watching me. She was lying back on her elbows;

enjoy the view of both the ocean and of me. Her face had changed and she seemed more peaceful then when we'd first arrived.

"What were you thinking about just then?" she asked me.

"Gosh," I said, "I don't know. Many things, I suppose."

"Tell me about them," she said as she leaned over onto her right side so she could face me better.

I didn't know where to begin, so I started with Auntie Melelani. I gave Kekoa a brief history of my childhood, and shared with her about the first time I'd seen hula dancers in Auntie's house. I told her about Auntie's love of *Hi'ilawe,* Queen Lili'u, and her collection of *tikis*. I told her about the *lei* I made for Auntie long ago, and about the bracelet she had given me most recently. K looked at my wrist and asked me why I wasn't wearing it. I told her I felt self-conscious; I wasn't Hawaiian, despite what Auntie had said, and I didn't want people to laugh at me.

"No one's going to laugh at you," K said. "Why would you think that? You really should wear it. It obviously means a lot to the both of you. And besides, it will make you fit right in. See?" she said as she pulled a gold chain out from beneath her t-shirt. "I've got one, too."

Kekoa wore a gold and black enamel pendent that hung from her chain. Her name was written in the same Old English scroll as my bracelet and was carved along the edges. The pendant was thin and flat, and it hung next to another charm I couldn't make out. I leaned in closer to take a look at both of the items, and that's when I saw the second one was a miniature golden Buddha encased in plastic. She held out the amulet for me to touch and examine, and then felt the need to explain.

"My family's Buddhist," she said somewhat reverently. "My uncle gave it to me a few years back. He's got his own board shop and everything. He's pretty cool."

"It's beautiful," I told her.

"Yeah," she paused. "It keeps me safe. You can come with me sometime to the temple if you want. I don't really go that often, but I'd be happy to show you."

I told her I would love to, and I agreed to start wearing my bracelet.

Chapter 18

There was a package waiting for me by the front door of the condo when I arrived home that night. Kekoa had dropped me off just as dusk was beginning to carpet itself over the island. Even though I'd slept in late that morning, I still felt exhausted. I had been through a rollercoaster of a day. Initially, I had woken up feeling wonderful. Then I had my first Jeffery sighting in weeks, followed by a very unforeseen and strange breakfast with Kekoa, and then an equally unplanned and beautiful afternoon with her out in the middle of nowhere. The feelings were conflicting, and my emotions were drained. The flip side of all this was that even though I felt overwhelmed, I didn't have just one thing to focus on or obsess about. Instead, I had many to choose from. That's probably why I was happy to have an early evening at home.

I picked up the small parcel leaning against the door and immediately recognized Auntie's beautiful cursive handwriting scrolled across the top of it. No one wrote like that anymore. I know I didn't, other than when I signed my name. I unlocked the door, kicked off my sandals, and plopped down onto the sofa. Using the jagged edge of my door key, I sliced along the sealing tape and opened the flaps of the box. Bubble wrap greeted me, and then an aroma that took me back to childhood. Auntie had overnight expressed homemade wontons across the Pacific Ocean! How precious was that?!

Leaning my head against the sofa, I laughed out loud at just how cute this little lady was. I thought about the role she'd played in my life's journey up to that point. If it hadn't been for her, there was no way I would have been sitting in that condo. Hawai'i wouldn't have even been on my radar, and the idea of moving to the islands would have sounded like nothing more than a tropical dream. My family had always been very generous, but they could have never given me this gift. It came from Auntie Melelani. *She* is the one who invited me into the land of gracefully powerful *mana* and deeply felt *aloha*. My world would forever be changed, as it already had been.

The beginning rumblings of a hungry stomach started to make themselves known, so I didn't even bother taking the box into the kitchen, but instead reached in and pulled out a wonton. Believe it or not, I could still smell the oil. Her gigantic wok coated the flaky treats with just the right amount of flavor, and they melted in my mouth just like when I was a kid. *This* was comfort food. Not grilled cheese, but wontons; and though I could have bought them just down the road, I know they wouldn't have tasted right. Of this, I had no doubt. Auntie had a special touch.

As I continued to munch my way through the greasy treats in the box, the quickness of my eating slowed down and the smile on my face began to drop. Tears welled up in the corner of my eyes, and I had to set the box down on the floor so I could wipe them with the back of my hand. No one was around, so I didn't bother trying to hold my emotions in, and instead I let myself have a good cry.

I wasn't sure what I was crying about. I just knew my shoulders were relaxing as I did. Shades of pink streaked themselves across the window opposite from where I was sitting; painting a sunset that dried my tears. I sat that way for a long time and started to breathe deeply, like I had done earlier in the day. Before long, I was calm. I pulled myself off the couch, picked up the box from the floor, and took it into the kitchen before the ants helped themselves to my package. Sadly, the tropics, unlike Seattle, invite all sorts of creatures into the house; something I never got used to no matter how hard I tried.

I wrapped the last of the wontons in paper towel and sealed them tightly in a plastic bag. They were my special reminders of home, and I wanted to make them last as long as I could. Opening the cupboard, I placed them on the top shelf so I wouldn't be tempted to eat them if I had a craving in the middle of the night. Then I washed my hands in the sink since they were greasy from the deep fried papers, and headed into my bedroom. There was something I had been meaning to do.

Tucked into the back corner of the closet was my large suitcase, the one I had come over from the mainland with. Inside, I kept a maroon velvet pouch where I hid all my valuables. I wasn't old enough to have acquired much, but the cross necklace my grandmother had given me, my passport, and some extra cash fit nicely inside the little bag. The gold bracelet from Auntie Mele was also tucked inside. I dragged the large case out onto the rug and unzipped it all the way around the front. When I opened the lid, I was surprised to see the gold bracelet had already fallen out of the little bag and had wedged itself into the corner of the suitcase. Thank goodness I hadn't lost it! Or maybe it had been simply trying to find its way to me. After the day I'd had, nothing would have surprised me.

Rolling the hem of my shirt into a ball, I used it to dust across the bangle that had been so beautifully etched and filled in with black enamel. It was magical to see my name shining back at me like that. Then I turned the bracelet slightly so I could once again read the inscription inside.

"You have a true love of the islands," it read in lovely flowing cursive.

I tried to remember which wrist Auntie wore her bracelet on, and then slipped the bangle onto my left arm. It fit perfectly. The weight of it was slightly heavy since I wasn't used to wearing it, but it made me feel grown up and mature. It made me feel like a woman; a woman filled with the Hawaiian spirit.

I walked over to the full length mirror and admired my reflection. Zeroing in on the beautiful gold, I imagined I was no different than the girls and women I'd been passing every day along the sidewalk.

Now I was truly one of them. Kekoa had promised no one would laugh at me, and I wanted to trust what she said was true. Despite her strangeness and her eagerness to take me everywhere the last couple of days, she had never misled me. So I tucked away any silly reservations I had about wearing it, and left the bangle to dangle as it pleased.

Chapter 19

"Hey! You made it," Kekoa hollered out across the floor of the somewhat vacant pub. Her hair was spiked more than usual, and there was a silver wallet chain hanging from the back pocket of her jeans that I had never seen before. K's bass guitar was strapped over her shoulder, and another girl was helping her push a large speaker across the stage. I walked over to where they were, feeling a little out of place, and hoped my attempt at concert-wear was suitable. Back home I hadn't been known for going out that much, so I wasn't exactly sure how I should dress. K immediately introduced me to one of her band members and then asked if I wanted something to drink. She pointed over to the bar located at the far side of the room and said Mo would hook me up with anything I wanted.

"Just tell him you're with me," she said confidently.

It was refreshing watching her take charge. Kekoa was focused. Unlike the few days prior when she seemed so out of it, this time she was in her element, and it showed.

Customers and friends started piling in shortly after I arrived, and the remaining two members, who were also girls, showed up just before the band was meant to go on. I stayed off to the side, hugging the stage, as K and the gals warmed up their equipment. But when the show was about to begin, panic set in; I wasn't sure what I was supposed to do. Thankfully, I felt a familiar tap on my right shoulder and was pleased to find Eddie standing there with a drink in his hand.

"We've got a table over on the other side," he told me. "Why don't you come join us?"

A wave of relief poured over me since I had no one to hang out with. I followed him through the crowd to the opposite side of the room, and was welcomed with an open seat when we arrived at the table. As I slid up onto the stool, the ceiling lights dimmed and the floodlight on the stage lit up. With a lone cord hanging in the air, the music set began.

K was in her own little world up there. She was on fire. The fiercest look of concentration never left her face through every song they played. She never giggled or smiled, didn't even interact with the audience. But she did strum her heart out. Her eyes stayed glued to the strings, and after each song finished she looked wiped out. Though the other girls were giving it their all, they didn't use as much energy. K, however, played with such passion that she looked obsessed by what she was doing. It was like she couldn't play hard enough.

When the set was over, the pub lights came back on and loud conversations started taking off. Eddie's friends introduced themselves to me, people I had never met before, and a couple bar girls brought a round of refills to our table. Since I didn't know anyone other than Eddie, I kept to myself and just listened. Two girls who'd already had way too much to drink began arguing about who had spent more time with Kekoa. I knew they weren't referring to coffee dates, but rather something more physical. The conversation began to make me feel uncomfortable, and at the same time I found myself feeling protective of my new friend. But I kept my mouth shut and just listened. I didn't say anything.

The person I'd spent the last week with didn't surface in the girls' talk about "hooking up." Instead, they described a very strange character who no one understood. Could this really be the same Kekoa? As far as I could tell, she'd never hit on me or anyone else when we were hanging out. And yet, according to the girls, she was a radiating "chick magnet," attracting all sorts of women – gay, straight, single and married. Even men hit on her from time to time. They described her as both bizarre and a flirt; claiming she had a dark side that acted as a barrier, shutting her off from any type of normal relationship. Women saw that as both frustrating and safe. It was hard for me to decipher who was being used more in this set up.

As the girls continued to chat about K's "skillful moves" and her "messed up demons," I became more and more disturbed by what I was hearing. I didn't like the way they were talking trash about her, and I also didn't like what I was learning. I knew to keep from jumping to conclusions; gossip is a deadly virus that can get out of control if it's allowed to. And so, I picked up my glass, spun around in my chair and looked out towards the crowd of people who were beginning to dance. I'd had enough of the groupies' chatter, and I knew it was better to shut out that noise than to keep on listening.

Not even five minutes passed before Kekoa joined us at our table. She looked like her old self; giggly and smoking. The girls who I'd been listening to earlier went from criticizing K to becoming all touchy-feely. They were all over her with done-up batting eyes, skirts that were dangerously too short, and compliments about her playing. At first I was disturbed, but then I tried not to laugh. These girls were such fools. K didn't brush them off completely, but she kept a cool demeanor around them. I just sat there watching. She looked over my way and gave me an upwards nod.

"What did you think?" she asked me, completely ignoring the others at the table.

Her face was lit up in anticipation of my approval, much like a little girl on Christmas morning. In that moment, all the crap I'd been listening to moments before just floated away, and the person I knew had once again returned.

"You guys were awesome!" I said as enthusiastically as I could. "Even better than the tape in your truck," I added with a wink.

"Yeah man. Wicked," she replied with a big smile of satisfaction. "Eh – your bracelet looks good," she said, pointing to my wrist. I gave a little smile in return.

The other girls just stood there, speechless and deflated. I'm sure they were wondering who the heck I was, and how I was connected to K. I thought it was satisfyingly funny.

"You want to get out of here?" she asked, making it clear she was up for leaving.

"Yeah, sure," I told her in return.

She quickly thanked everyone for stopping by, waved to Eddie, who had been sitting at the table next to us for the last half hour, and grabbed my hand. Like at the water's edge a few days before, her touch was gentle and comforting, and didn't at all fit in with the environment around us. The moment was conflicting: loud music, tight miniskirts, and lots of alcohol verses a kind and tender gesture. She didn't say anything to me, but led us through the crowd towards the door. Mo waved from the bar and flashed us a pearly smile as we passed by his way, and once we were outside, she let go of my hand.

"I need a drink," she said, as she looked off towards the right. I was confused.

"Why don't we just get one here?" I asked her.

"Too many people," she said, still looking away from me. "My head was getting fuzzy."

I quietly stood there; waiting to follow her lead and unclear about what she wanted to do. She pulled out a pack of cigarettes and lit one up. Her initial exhale was long and drawn out, like a sigh of relief or surrender. Still waiting, I adjusted my tank top and pulled my hair back behind my ears. I couldn't stand the silence any longer.

"Thanks, again, for inviting me to come out tonight," I began to ramble. "It was really great to see your band play. You guys have a lot of talent."

"Yeah, thanks," she said. "And, thanks for coming."

Within in a matter of minutes, Kekoa had gone from giggly in the pub to distant in the street. Her eyes were glossed over, and she once again had that faraway look I'd seen on the rocks. She kept staring out into the darkness at nothing in particular. Not once did she look me in the eye after coming out the door of the pub. Where had she gone?

"Are you ok?" I hesitantly asked her. "If you need to go or something, that's cool."

She took another long drag of her cigarette and flicked the ash onto the sidewalk. Her face was in deep thought. Finally she turned her head my direction, with her eyes following just a fraction of second behind. Ever so carefully she looked at me and then delicately picked her words.

"I think maybe I should catch up with you later," she said. "If that's ok with you?"

"Yeah, of course," I tried to reassure her. "Everything ok?" I asked once more.

"Yeah, yeah," she replied. "I just need to go. You going to be ok by yourself?" she asked, not that I think any answer would have made much difference.

"Sure, of course," I smiled back. "I'm sure Eddie can give me a lift home."

"Ok, cool," she said. "See ya around," and she headed down the sidewalk.

I watched her walk away until I could no longer see her figure under the street light. I stood there for a moment after she was gone. Something wasn't right, and though I didn't know what it was, I could feel it. I took a deep breath, pushed open the door to the pub, and went in search of Eddie. It was time he and I had our little talk.

Chapter 20

Eddie wasn't much help. I tried asking him what the deal was with Kekoa, after describing the incident that had just taken place outside the pub. He didn't seem bothered by it. Instead, he shrugged it off and told me to give her a little space; she'd be fine in the morning. I couldn't make out whether Eddie knew something he didn't want to tell me, or if he thought I was overacting to nothing. I dropped the subject, but something still didn't sit right with me.

Midterm exams were coming up, and I had a ton of reading to catch up on. Instead of coming home in the middle of the day, I thought it might be wise to hang out on campus and study; the environment might help me be able to focus. I laid my bag down under a large banyan tree, sheltering myself from the bright sun, then proceeded to pull out my text book while hunting around for a yellow highlighter. I didn't know if I would get much done, but it was worth a try.

It was the middle of the afternoon, and the heat wasn't letting up any. My stomach started to rumble, reminding me I'd forgotten to eat that morning, and I knew it was pointless to ignore the cravings; there was no way I could concentrate while I was hungry. Still seated on the grass, I looked around for the closest food stand. Just across the way was a coffee cart, complete with pastries and a basket of fruit. Good enough, I thought.

Since I had just gotten myself all settled under the tree, I didn't want to lose my spot nor have to pack everything up again. I figured it was just a few feet away, and I could leave my things where they were, so I grabbed my wallet and quickly walked over to the cart.

Luck was on my side; there were no customers in line. I was about to pick up a jumbo chocolate chip cookie when my eye caught notice of the glass container holding steamed buns and dim sum. Ever since arriving on the island, I had steered clear of such Asian treats, but watched so many others devour them with great pleasure. There was something about the smell of the dim sum that made me turn up my nose. I just couldn't take it. But the white sticky buns with little red dots on top looked like they might be ok. The woman working the cart told me my choices were down to barbeque pork or sweet cream. I decided to be brave; I ordered one of each. Using metal tongs as to not burn her hands, she carefully lifted them from the bamboo tray. I could see the steam rising from their centers.

"Be careful your mouth," she warmed me, "they gonna be real hot!"

Assuring her I would, I took the plastic bag from her hand. I handed over a couple of dollars and was putting the change in the side zipper pocket of my wallet when a voice I knew well completely startled me.

"Those are the best, man," Kekoa affirmed, standing there with her backpack over her shoulder. "*Manapua* are my favorite."

"What are you doing here," I asked cautiously.

After the episode from the night before, I wasn't sure what kind of mood to expect from her. This stalker-like coincidence of running into her caught me off guard, plus it felt like it was becoming a habit.

K said she'd just gotten out of class and saw me standing there; that's all. Fair enough. Maybe I was being too sensitive. She seemed like her normal self, minus a cigarette, so I invited her to come join me under the tree. She told me she was on her way out, but would walk with me for a minute. By the time we reached the banyan tree, however, she had already pulled out a pack of smokes and had obviously changed her mind about leaving. Sliding out of her flip-flops, she sat on the ground cross-legged. I noticed the day's t-shirt was once again black, but featured a red and green skull on the front. *Festive*, I sarcastically thought to myself.

I didn't want there to be an elephant in the room between us, so I went ahead and brought up the night before.

"Everything turn out ok last night?" I asked.

"Yeah man," she said, "Sorry I had to bail on ya. I met up with some chicks downtown. We drank way too much," she laughed, "and I guess one of them brought me home. I wasn't sure I was going to make it to campus today."

She thought it was funny, but I wasn't laughing.

"Listen, though," she said, blowing smoke in the opposite direction of where I was sitting, "I asked around and found out where that original gold bracelet is on display – the one you were telling me about. We can go check it out if you want. And afterwards I can take you to the Lili'uokalani statue. I think you'll like it. It's not that far."

Once again she surprised me. K had done *research* for *me*? When we first met I know I told her about some of these things, but I had no clue she had taken them to heart. Not only that, she looked into them on her own accord. I was speechless and deeply touched. I softened my guarded demeanor and thanked her, saying I would love to go with her sometime.

"What are you doing tomorrow?" she asked, "Cuz I'm going to the temple in the morning, and you could come with me then. Afterwards we could go in search of the bracelet and Queen Lili'u."

Her requests to have me join her were always immediate. Why the rush? We had all the time in the world, but to her these activities needed to be carried out right away. I noticed this same urgency the day we visited the sea and each time she invited me to come watch her band perform. There wasn't anything wrong with it, but it did seem rather odd.

We agreed to meet at the Koi Café the next morning around 7am. Apparently temple visiting is best if it's done early in the day. Noa sent us on our way with coffee in to-go cups and a couple bagels for the drive. K drove up through the Pali, whose majestic mountains always surrounded me with awe, and this time we kept the radio turned off. Mist clouded the trucks windows, creating a feeling of reverence before we even arrived. Once we reached the other side of the island, Kekoa pointed out areas where she used to hang out, including the street leading to her parents' house. We never went there, though.

She turned the truck down a one way gravel road, where red and gold ornaments adorned a Buddhist temple nestled among the trees. It was beautiful. I had never visited a temple before, so I wasn't sure about the protocol on where to go or what to do; Kekoa would be my guide. We each jumped out of the car, and before I closed the door she told me it was ok to leave my bag in the cab, so I did. As we reached the front steps, K took off her shoes and put them on the bottom stair; I placed mine right next to hers. We entered the building and she walked over to a small table piled with candles, incense, and *leis*. I didn't follow her, but instead waited next to the door. When she returned, her hands were full of the beautiful items. She handed me an orange candle and three incense sticks bound together with a rubber band. A small piece of paper was sticking out of them.

"What's this?" I asked her.

"Gold," she replied. "I'll show you."

Kekoa draped one of the floral *leis* over my arm and led me into the largest chamber of the building. From the outside, it was hard to see the Buddha in the middle of the room, but once we entered the great hall, I was taken aback. The largest gold Buddha I had ever seen was seated on the floor, cross-legged, and ever so slightly smiling down on us. The look of immense peace on His lips was breathtaking. I just kept staring up at Him.

"Wow," I said with a great sigh.

"First time?" K asked, with a tender smile.

"Yeah," I told her. "I'd seen pictures before, but nothing up close like this." I kept looking up at Him while still holding my incense and *lei*. "It's a bit overwhelming... but, in a good way."

"Here, come follow me," she said and we walked over to a large lantern burning oil.

She took the rubber band off the bundle and said I should do the same. Turning her three incense sticks upside down, Kekoa dipped the ends into the flame and waited for them to ignite. Without letting them burn too far, she removed the sticks from the fire and then briskly shook them in the air to extinguish the flame, releasing the smoke before turning them back upright. Nodding her head for me to mirror her, she then lit the candle.

I was doing my best to follow her example, but was having a hard time holding everything together in my hands. This was getting complicated. I was so worried I would drop something – much like the tea incident at Jeffery's – that I started to bite the inside of my cheek. Kekoa was patient and offered to help me light my candle.

All lit and ready to proceed, we quietly walked to the front of the Buddha. No one else was in the temple except the two of us, which I was thankful for since it helped me to relax. A long iron bar holding similar golden candles like the ones in our hands was placed at the Buddha's feet next to two copper barrels full of sand. Each held the remains of used incense sticks; long red threads that stuck out like dried grass, representing the prayers of those who had come before us.

Holding the end of her candle over the top of another, K melted the bottom and then tried to secure it to the iron rod. The first attempt failed, so she simply tilted it, causing hot wax to drip like melted gold, and immediately glued the end to the liquid. This time it stayed, and I followed suit.

Carefully, Kekoa knelt down on the hardwood floor. She waited for me to secure my candle and join her before moving on. I knelt down next to her and smiled, signaling I was ready to continue. Placing the ends of the sticks between her palms, she showed me how to form my hands into the shape of a lotus bud without dropping the incense. Gently, she held them out in front of her, right above her heart. She'd already tucked the three little pieces of tan paper between two small fingers, and she did her best not to laugh at me as I attempted to do the same.

"You can pray to Him," she gestured towards the Buddha, "about whatever you want."

Then she looked away and dropped her head slightly, but she never closed her eyes.

I wasn't really sure how to pray to a golden Buddha, nor did I know what He stood for. Yet surprisingly, I was comfortable. I went with the flow and imagined the universe was open for business and ready to commune with me. Closing my eyes, I allowed the sweet scent of the incense to surround me. Only one thought appeared in my mind: *please guide me and bless me.*

Sitting on the floor with Kekoa was one the most peaceful moments of my life. There were no distractions, no noises, and no worries surrounding us. Candles continued to burn, some on their last tongues of flame, and I didn't want to move when K eventually stirred. She stood up and placed her incense sticks – which had burned halfway down – into the sand before draping the *lei* over the Buddha's lap. From between her fingers she opened the small papers and showed me the tiny squares of gold foil hidden inside. Walking around the back of the Buddha, she pressed the gold squares onto the statue in three different places, careful not to get any on her fingers. A trash basket along the wall collected the discarded papers. When she was finished she placed her lotus shaped palms in front of her face once more and bowed slightly towards the Buddha. Then it was my turn.

"Does it matter where I put the gold," I asked her.

"No," she said. "It's up to you. For me, I always put it in the same three places: His foot, so He'll show me where to go in life; His hand, so He'll help me be nice to others; and His back, so He'll protect me."

What a beautiful way to pray, I thought, and I ended up doing the same. Kekoa stood near me as I walked around the Buddha, silently taking my slips of paper when I was finished with each of them. She placed them into the basket and then reached up towards my hair.

"Stand still," she said.

Delicately, she pinched a small speck of gold out from a few stray strands and laid it in my hand.

How in the world did I manage to get gold in my hair? I had been trying so hard to be careful. She could tell I was embarrassed, and in turn gave me the most tender of smiles.

"I guess you're just extra blessed," she said

Her words were divine. We stood there for a moment, looking at one another, and neither of us said a thing. The world slowed down, and even my heart was nothing more than a very soft flutter. It was just the Buddha, Kekoa, and me. Nothing else mattered; not the past nor the future, only the moment itself. We were one with the world. We were Elsewhere.

"Thank you," I said to her from the deepest part of my soul.

"You're welcome," she replied, never once moving her eyes away from mine.

Chapter 21

I knew the day was going to be one I wouldn't forget. From the spectacular sunrise in the early morning, the mystical drive through the *mauna*, mountains, of the Pali, and the deeply spiritual encounter at the Buddhist temple – how could it not?

In the time it took for only a few hours to pass, my world had transitioned once again; only this time it was vertical instead of horizontal. I didn't walk into a new chapter, but rather, stepped deeper into the one I was already living. My senses were heightened; from the squawking sounds of tropical birds to the whispers along my arm from the light breeze. I felt alive, truly alive. It was the same feeling Jeffery described from reading certain passages in books. I wanted to cry, I wanted to laugh, and I didn't know why. I felt I had stumbled upon the key to the universe. What it was, however, I couldn't tell you.

Kekoa and I pulled up in front of the famous Bishop Museum and realized we were famished. The bagels from earlier that morning were only going to tie us over for so long. Down the walk a ways, a sweet little old man was pouring rainbow colored syrup over the largest snow cones of shaved ice imaginable. K and I both noticed them at the same time, and then looked at each other with silly grins.

"Shall we?" I asked, hopefully.

"Yeah, man!" she replied with great approval.

In my time on the island, I had come to believe shaved ice was the ideal meal. I suppose it couldn't technically be called food, but it satisfied better than anything else I knew. It was sweet, refreshing, cool, and filling. I ended up with five different flavors all bleeding into each other on my cone; Kekoa stood steadfast with just lychee.

Rehydrated and ready to move into some much needed air conditioning, K paid for two tickets to the museum, and we were on our way. Red and yellow feathered capes lined the walls, and wooden bowls that once held Hawaii's favorite staple, *poi*, were proudly on display. Such items of the *ali'i*, royalty, looked so simple, yet held great *mana* and importance. A few even shocked me, like the massive necklaces made from human hair adorned with real bone. I admit, I was relieved Queen Lili'uokalani had a slightly different taste in jewelry.

Eventually we made our way around to where the prized bangle was laid out. K and I walked most of the museum together up till then, but I steered off the path when the bracelet caught my eye. Like a pilgrim on her way to a sacred site, I slowly moved in closer to get a better look.

The bracelet was old and well worn. At first I thought it was broken, but then realized it was simply a different style. The black enamel on the surface was fading, yet still readable. "*Aloha 'Oe*," it read. I whispered the words out loud.

"It means 'farewell to thee'," K explained as she walked up next to me. "The bracelet was a gift from Lili'u to her assistant. Not long after, she was dethroned and no longer Queen."

"That's so sad," I soberly replied.

"Yeah," K answered and then looked off to the left; I turned back to take another look at the bracelet. "It's the same as her famous song, you know?" K asked.

I had no idea what she was referring to and told her as much. K ran her hand through her hair and twisted one of the piercings in her ear. She looked uncomfortable.

"*Aloha 'Oe* is a song Lili'u wrote," she said. "People sing it when someone leaves, especially if they die. It's totally famous, but I don't really like it, though," she expressed while gripping the back of her neck with her hand. "It's too haunting. But it's really famous."

As I stood there watching and listening to Kekoa, I realized she always did two things around me: (1) she went out of her way to explain island culture, from its history to its quirks, regardless of whether she was interested in it or not, and (2) she quietly cried out for help. I could tell something was wrong; I could see she wasn't at peace. What was hurting her?

Suddenly, in classic Kekoa fashion, she shifted once again and brought light back into the conversation.

"Some people believe Lili'u's *Aloha 'Oe* also means '*forever love*.' I guess the two meanings go together," she kept rambling. I didn't want to interrupt her, so I stayed quiet. "Like if you're telling someone goodbye and you really care about them, you know? Then I guess what *Aloha 'Oe* really means is that it doesn't matter where they are, you will still love them; your love goes with them." We both thought about her words. "Dang," she paused, "that kind of goodbye must hurt like hell."

"Yeah," I thought out loud, "you're right. That kind of goodbye would be a huge loss."

We let the silence hang in the air for a moment before she asked me if I was ready to leave. There was still a lot more museum to see, but I could tell she needed out of the building.

The minute we reached the fresh air and afternoon sun, K lit up a cigarette and sat down on the curb. Her foot was shaking a bit and she kept squinting her eyes; both of us had left our sunglasses in the truck. She looked like she needed some space, so I walked around the gardens next to the museum, pressing my face in close to the fragrant blossoms. I closed my eyes and breathed in all the beauty of their scent. There's really nothing else quite like it – God's tropical perfume.

When I returned to the truck, K was already inside with her shades on and music blasting. She looked better.

"I just love the smell of those flowers," I told her, pointing in the direction of the plumeria trees as I got in the cab.

"Flowers!" she said, pointing at me as if she was on a mission. "Great idea," and we were off.

Chapter 22

Floral *leis* can be found virtually anywhere in Hawai'i, so I didn't understand why Kekoa was driving us a far distance just to buy the same thing that we could have gotten down the road. We were in search of *leis* to take with us to Queen Lili'u's statue. But not just any *leis*; they had to be the right kind, and Kekoa said her Auntie Marian would know what we needed.

Like with Melelani, Marian wasn't actually related to K. "Auntie" was a term of respect given to those who were older. Outside a shop no larger than the size of my bathroom, sat the cutest little lady I had ever seen. She was tiny, with callused hands, a woven straw hat, and a twinkling smile.

"Kekoa!" she cried out in a burst of joy upon seeing us get out of the truck. She didn't get up from the mat she was sitting on, but rather threw open her arms, ready to embrace her "niece." I couldn't stop smiling.

"Hey, Auntie," K replied, carefully giving Marian a hug that wouldn't crush her delicate frame.

"And who is this?" she asked, motioning for me to come give her a hug as well.

Her delight in meeting me couldn't have been more genuine. After the hugging and introductions had been taken care of, we flicked off our shoes and joined Auntie on the mat. Once again K sat cross-legged, much like the golden Buddha, I now realized. She told Auntie we were on our way to visit Lili'u – making it sound as if she were a live person and not just a statue – and that we needed her to help with the *leis*.

"Oh, of course!" Auntie exclaimed, "Most definitely. Now you two wait right here."

She slowly gathered herself up from the ground and walked into the store. We could hear her rumbling around and offered to help, but she insisted she was fine. After a few minutes, Auntie Marian emerged from the shop carrying an armload of supplies: long needles, string, purple ribbon, and a plastic bag full of lavender and white blossoms.

"Crown flowers," she answered my quizzical look. "Flowers fit for a Queen," and she slowly lowered herself back down onto the mat. "This is her *favorite* flower," Auntie said romantically, drawing out the word favorite. "And you know, she loves purple," she added, as if I'd already known.

She handed K and I each a twelve-inch long needle and a length of string. We threaded the needles, following Auntie's lead, and proceeded to string the blossoms one after the other.

"*Leis* of *aloha*," Auntie said, "are the signature of the islands. Everybody loves *leis*," she continued with a slight giggle. "You know," she started in again like she was telling me a secret, "sometimes at the end of the day I make a *lei* just for fun, and then on my way home I walk up to a stranger and put it on them! Ha ha!" she laughed, clapping her hands. "They are always so surprised. But you know," she looked me in the eye with hers twinkling, "they always smile." And with that she clapped her hands again.

Kekoa giggled, and I grinned so big my cheeks hurt. Auntie Marian was adorable.

"You know why I do that?" she asked while piercing the needle through another crown flower, "because *that* is what the *aloha spirit* is all about; giving love to people you don't know, just to make them smile. Maybe they had a bad day or got terrible news, and my *lei* brought them a moment of hope. Or maybe they already felt on top of the world, and my little gift confirmed it. It's not my job to know why, but it *is* my job to *do*." With that, she sighed and stopped threading for a moment. Her eyes teared up and she wiped them with her hand. K and I both stopped working on our *leis*, too, and waited.

"Oh silly me," Auntie said, trying to reassure us with a recovering smile. "It's just that everyone knows what *aloha means*, but so many have forgotten how to *live* it." She put down her needle and thread, and reached out to both of us with her hands.

"Don't ever forget," she said, looking deeply into each of our faces, and then she tightened the grip on our hands and zapped us with her strength and her energy. This little woman radiated the spirit she was talking about.

She let go of us and returned to her *lei* making.

"Oh yes," she announced approvingly, "Lili'u is going to love these. She, too, was full of the *aloha spirit*. And her faith in God was strong as a rock. Whoa!" she said with great enthusiasm, "did she ever have *mana*! Rest her soul. She fought for us. She loved her people fiercely; talk about a strong woman in a man's world. Bless her soul."

I remembered Auntie Mele saying something similar about Lili'u "bursting with *mana*," and I thought about her famous song of *Aloha*. She clearly was a special woman.

When our *leis* were complete, Auntie Marian tied purple ribbons to each and draped all three over my left arm. As she did, she noticed my gold bracelet. Rubbing her finger over the engraving, Auntie sweetly said my name. She looked at me, her eyes still twinkling, and she touched my cheek.

"Please give my *lei* to Lili'u, won't you dear?" she asked. I promised I would.

Gently, Auntie took Kekoa's hand and walked us to the truck. She hugged K one last time and then placed her two hands on K's face. Both of them closed their eyes, and Auntie whispered something up at K; Kekoa was at least a foot taller. She leaned down so Auntie could reach, and Marian kissed the top of Kekoa's head. The gesture was slow and sweet, and when they pulled away, each of them had tears in their eyes. Kekoa tried to look away, but Auntie held her face once more and stared deeply into her. They were peaceful, and silently Kekoa nodded. Auntie smiled.

"Ok now," she said, "it's time you girls be on your way. Lili'u's waiting."

We piled into the cab, carefully laying the flowers over my lap.

"*Mahalo*, Auntie," K said to Marian. I believe she was thanking her for more than just the *leis*. I waved goodbye, and we headed back down the dirt road to the highway.

Traffic was steady as we reached the city. We lucked out finding a parking spot right next to the state capital building. Beautiful lush trees surrounded us, including a banyan tree larger than any I'd seen before.

"Right over there is *'Iolani Palace*," K told me as she pointed across my shoulders. "*'Iolani* means heavenly hawk, which is a symbol of the *ali'i*, or royalty. The palace is where Lili'u lived." Again, I felt like someone on a pilgrimage.

K carefully lifted the three *leis* from my lap so I could get out of the truck, and then handed them back to me. I was trying to delicately handle all of them and grab my bag, when K came to the rescue.

"I've got it," she said, and she swung the strap over her shoulder. "This way," she motioned for us to head off through the park of trees. Birds called to one another as we walked among the long strings hanging from the branches. The sun was warm, but not too hot, and there didn't seem to be many people venturing around. We turned a corner, protected by a guard and an iron gate, and then there she was.

The six-foot tall statue stood alone as the sun shone down upon her. She appeared stoic and strong. Gifts of *leis* and single cut flowers had already been left by previous pilgrims and admirers, and a tiny bird was perched on her hand. We ceremoniously circled around her and read the inscriptions etched in stone at the base. Running my hand over her name, I thought of Auntie Mele. Could she feel this moment with me? For some reason, I believed she could.

I handed K one of the *leis* and placed the other two over Lili'u's arm. K added hers right after.

"*Aloha*," I whispered while looking up at her, "and thank you."

Auntie Marian was right; Lili'u was a strong woman in a man's world. I also knew she was dark skinned and cheated by a pale skinned conqueror. She had been unfairly wronged, and yet through it all she never abandoned the three gems she wore steadfastly in her glorious crown: *aloha*, *mana*, and her faith in God. Nothing could take them away from her, and no one ever did. She was a strong woman, all right – a woman among women; an example for us all.

When I finished paying my respects to Queen Lili'u, I noticed Kekoa was gone. In the shade of the walkway overhang, I found her; cigarette in hand and a distant look in her eyes. I sat down on the bench next to her, and we stayed like that for some time. It had been a long day.

Two little birds played together on the ground in front of us; flying back and forth until eventually they flew away. The sky was ever so slightly beginning to change color as it prepared for evening, and eventually we both stood up and walked back to the truck. This time I carried my own bag.

"Thanks for today," I said, putting on my seatbelt.

"Yeah sure, no problem," K replied with a slight soberness in her voice.

Downtown was beginning to get its second wind with tourists heading out for dinner and street lights coming alive. However, I'd had enough for one day. I asked K to take me home and thanked her before heading into the lobby of the condo. Looking down at my arms, I noticed my skin had gotten a bit of color, so I wasn't paying any attention to where I was going. That's when I ran into Jeffery.

He and I rounded the corner about the same time, but thankfully he saw me coming. His manicured hands braced me before we had an embarrassing collision.

"Oh my gosh! I'm sorry," I instinctively called out.

"No, no. Not at all," Jeffery replied. "Are you ok?" he asked with deep concern.

"Yes, I'm fine." I responded, somewhat flustered.

"Here," Jeffery gestured towards the lobby couch. "Come sit down."

I nodded and sat across the coffee table from him. It had been a long time since we'd seen each other, and so much had changed. I was no longer hurt or angry, yet I wasn't sure I wanted to start something with him again. I wasn't even sure I wanted to be having this conversation. Residents continued to walk past us in the lobby, and a few looked over our way.

"How have you been?" he asked.

"Fine," I said. "I've been fine." He nodded, holding his hands properly in his lap.

"I had been wanting to…"

"You know, Jeffery," I interrupted, running my hand over my eyes, "I'm sorry, but I've had a really long day. I just can't do this right now."

He sat up straighter than he already was and inhaled deeply.

"Of course. I'm sorry," he said. "Perhaps another-time."

"Ok," I replied, giving him a small smile, and

then I left. My day had been so full, and there were too many thoughts and emotions already floating around inside me. I honestly couldn't deal with anything more. Though part of me was thrilled Jeffery wanted to see me, another part was confused; I wasn't sure whether Jeffery was meant to be involved in this chapter of my life or not. The fact that I was questioning it was both surprising and liberating. Perhaps I had truly moved on.

Chapter 23

I needed advice, so I decided to write Auntie Mele; she would know what to do. My weekly letters home to her had started to stretch out into monthly notes, if I was lucky. It had been awhile since I'd put pen to paper and gotten in touch with her, but that didn't mean she hadn't been in my thoughts. In fact, I thought of Auntie all the time. Moving to Hawai'i taught me that no matter where I went in this world, and no matter how long I was gone, the people most dear to me would always be there when I returned. If they weren't, then it was probably for the best. I also learned that the ones who love us the most seem to go with us, traveling close by, tucked away in little pockets of our hearts. These realizations gave me a great deal of comfort during my time on the island, and I prayed the experience was mutual. I wanted Auntie to feel me with her as well.

I sealed the envelope and dropped it in the mailbox outside the condo complex, knowing I would hear back from Auntie by the end of the week. She was always good that way.

The day was sunny and bright, as usual, and tourist season was slowing down slightly; there weren't as many people packed together onto the beaches. As I walked along the sidewalk, I recognized a few of the locals heading my way. We smiled at each other as we passed; clearly they'd seen me before, too. I no longer felt like a new guest in Hawai'i, but I didn't feel like it was home yet either. Surprisingly, Kekoa had been right when she said the simple act of wearing my bracelet would help me fit right in. Not only did I look like the women of O'ahu, but I actually felt the part.

I popped my head into the nearest ABC store, knowing I could find another just a few yards away. ABC in Hawai'i was like Starbucks back home; stand on one corner and you could see another not that far from you. I headed to the cosmetics aisle and picked out some silver nail polish. My toes were in major need of pampering and care, but I refused to pay the outrageous prices salons charged tourists. So, for the time being, self-painted pedicures were on the menu. I looked at my watch and saw I had just enough time to catch the bus; I didn't want to be late.

The boys had invited me to check out their favorite new lunch spot: *Mama's Noodles*. They claimed "Mama's" broth was the best on the whole island. I'd been hearing about this place almost daily since they discovered it, and agreed to join them on my day off from school. Noa's cousin, Jay, had made me a map earlier at breakfast, and in the end it was so simple I could have found it on my own. The guys were already onto their second bowl of noodles and laughing it up when I arrived. Down at the end of the table I saw Kekoa; we waved. One of the guys pulled up a plastic stool for me to sit on, and I squeezed in between them.

The little noodle shop was quaint and simple. Completely outdoors, the only protection it had from the rain was care of the plastic awning under the trees. Ten metal tables filled the small space, along with "Mama's" lone noodle cart, where she had all the fixings to personalize one's bowl. That was it. There were no menus or placemats, just a box of chopsticks and spoons at the end of the cart. I don't even think there were napkins. The place was packed with locals, nearby shop owners, and kids on their lunch breaks. My guess was most tourists wouldn't have thought to venture in.

The first thing Noa did was add two spoonfuls of sugar to the broth in my bowl.

"Sugar?" I asked, making a face, clearly questioning his judgment.

"Trust me," he said with relaxed confidence.

Obviously, he knew what he was talking about. These noodles were awesome. Noa showed me how to pick them out of the soup using chopsticks, and then place them into the spoon in my other hand. Then I carefully dipped the whole thing back into the bowl for some broth. It was a dance of the utensils. As I looked around me I wondered, why is it that the most unexpected places bring the most delight?

As the guys finished, seats started to open up all around the table. I moved my bowl down a few chairs so I could be near Kekoa. She had been quiet through lunch, other than waving when I first got there, and we hadn't said much.

"Where you goin' after this?" I asked her.

"Not sure, man," she said. "Why, what's up?"

"I thought maybe we could go check out more of your secret hot spots," I answered.

"We could do that," she replied, while placing her chopsticks on top of the bowl to show she was finished. "But I have to make a stop first."

Most of the crew had left by the time I was done eating, but K didn't seem to mind waiting. She was patient with me and in no hurry.

When she started up the truck, I asked her where she needed to go, and she told me we were going to make a quick stop by the craft store. I tried not to laugh. That was the *last* thing I thought she would say, and sure enough, we were on our way to the yarn department.

"Are you working on a project?" I asked, still thrown for a loop by all this.

"Something like that," she replied, as she reached up for a ball of light blue yarn. She rolled the wool between her fingers and appeared satisfied. "This will work," she said, and then headed to the checkout counter.

Her interaction with the clerk was kind and respectful, and again I thought about how odd the scene was. Her outward appearance truly didn't match the person inside. It was bizarre; and now she was buying yarn.

K took me to another beach, one that was just enough away from the big hotels. A few sunbathers were already lathered up in oil, but for the most part it was deserted. I threw my bag over my shoulder and shut the door of the truck. Kekoa was messing around in the cab for a few minutes, so I leaned against the side and waited. The breeze was full and strong, blowing my hair back away from my face, and I could smell the sea. When I heard K's door close, I started out towards the water.

"Come over this way," she told me, and I followed her to an area of gigantic boulders piled over the sand.

We climbed up onto them, and then back down the other side. This time I was able to handle the rocks by myself. K cautiously turned her head back a time or two, just to make sure, and then went ahead. She'd led me to a tiny cove, hidden from where we'd just been standing.

"I love it!" I called out, smiling as I looked around me. "It's like our own private island."

"Yep," Kekoa said proudly, "I know. I like to come here sometimes to get away. And right over there," she pointed out towards the coral reefs, off the tip of the rocks, "is where the sharks gather."

"Really?!" I asked, my eyes widening.

"Yeah," K answered, nodding her head.

We plopped ourselves down onto the sand, and I rummaged through my bag trying to find the nail polish I'd just bought. I moved my sunglasses from my face to the top of my head, trying to get a better look inside.

"You can read or whatever," K said.

"I was thinking about painting my nails," I replied. K giggled.

"You're cute," she said.

I looked at her, my glasses still on top of my head.

"I am?" I asked.

"Yeah," she replied, then look back out towards the ocean.

Reaching down into the bottom of my bag, I eventually found the small bottle of silver polish. I hiked my right knee up to my chest and began to paint my toes. Kekoa watched.

"You know," I continued, without taking my eyes off my foot, "I could paint yours when I'm finished."

"Nooooo, no, no, no, no," she defended herself. This time I was the one laughing.

The wind off the water was ideal, drying my nails so quickly I didn't have to wait to apply a second coat. As I dipped the brush back into the jar, a bit of light blue caught the corner of my eye. It was a piece of the yarn K had purchased earlier. She was tying it to something and trying to untangle the string.

"I have to go visit my uncle tomorrow," she said, still dealing with the yarn since the wind kept tossing it around. "He lives over on one of the small islands. Remember, I told you about him?"

I honestly couldn't remember, but I nodded anyway.

"You can come with me if you want," she continued. "It's just one night, and my uncle's really cool. He's nothing like Waikiki."

There was that urgency of hers again. I told her I'd think about it. She said, "ok," and then got up and walked down to the waves.

My toes were still drying from their second coat of paint, which took longer than the first, so I laid back and closed my eyes. The sand was warm on my back and the sun was pleasant on my face. When I sat back up, I had to squint my eyes to see clearly. Kekoa was standing knee deep in the waves, and it looked like she was dragging something through the water. What in the world was she doing, I wondered. I pulled my glasses back down to my face, and my eyes adjusted. From my short distance away, I could see the light blue of the string; she was pulling it. Kekoa continued to walk back and forth along the sand, sometimes stepping out further into the waves. I stayed seated where I was on the shore, watching.

Eventually she and her light blue string made their way to the waters right in front of me.

"What are you doing?" I called out to her.

"Walking my fish," she said very matter of fact. I laughed.

"You're crazy," I shouted back, still laughing. "You know, sometimes I really worry about you."

I hung my comment out in the air for her to catch. I thought for sure she'd make a joke or laugh along. But she didn't. She just kept walking, and the little blue string followed along beside her.

Chapter 24

I was packed and ready to go, sitting on the curb outside the condo when the sun began to rise over the Hawaiian islands. The morning was calm and peaceful, and the waves were swelling, full of surfers trying to a catch a big one. Somewhere out there were my friends, living on the edge of their boards and smiling the whole way.

As I waited for the sight of Kekoa's familiar truck, I checked my handbag to make sure I had enough cash with me. As I rummaged around, I pulled out the bottle of silver nail polish from the day before. Tangled around it was a sea-weathered piece of blue yarn. Kekoa must have put it in my bag, or it somehow got thrown in there by accident. I held it in my hand, thoughtfully, and replayed the afternoon from the hidden cove in my head.

Two headlights came up over the hill, so I brushed the memory away and tossed the string back into my bag. A white four-door car pulled up next to the curb, with Kekoa's head hanging out the passenger's window; a pretty guarded looking guy with skull tattoos on both his arms was driving.

"Hey!" Kekoa drew out the word. "Sorry we're late. The truck wouldn't start this morning. Happens sometimes."

She opened the passenger's door and picked up my duffle bag, gently placing it on the back seat and then inviting me in. I crawled in the back, directly behind where K had been sitting, and noticed the driver watching me. Kekoa closed the door and jumped back up front.

"This is Tony," she said. "He's taking us to the island."

"Hi," I said, trying to look friendly. Tony just nodded. Not really a big talker, I guess.

"You hungry?" K asked, turning around in her seat.

"I'm ok," I told her, but I was secretly thrilled when she asked Tony to pull over so she could buy some *manapua* from the vendor by the side of the road.

We drove around the coast, enjoying our breakfast, and Kekoa began messing with the radio. She found a station she liked and cranked the volume. All four windows were rolled down, the sea breeze was flying through the car, and we were on our way. It dawned on me that no one knew I was leaving O'ahu for a couple days, not even Noa. I was truly escaping from everyone and everything. A flutter of excitement rushed through me; I felt liberated.

An average size speed boat met us at the marina, and Kekoa carried my bag on board along with her own. Tony zipped up his jacket and pushed the boat away from the dock. He knew something I didn't; early morning on the sea can be very cold.

My hair was flying all over the place when we first sped out of the marina. Quickly I found a clip in my duffle bag and tied it up. Strands of hair kept falling out, but it was better than nothing.

K moved up to the front of the boat's open bow and sat back into the padded booth. Her sunglasses covered her eyes, so I couldn't read her expression very well. From what I could tell, she looked tired or in deep thought. The trip across the water took longer than I'd expected, but eventually we came upon a sandy beach, vacant of sunbathers or tourists. The island was lush and green, and in front of us sat a small house perched up on wooden stilts. A tall dark man with a gentle face and *ti*-leaf bandana waited for us on the shore. Tony turned off the engine and we floated the rest of the way in. As the waves pushed our boat one final time inward, we landed, and the man on the beach smiled from ear to ear.

"*Aloha, keiki,*" he said, looking at Kekoa.

"*Aloha*, Fred," she called back.

The man walked out to the boat and helped tie it to a large rock. Kekoa jumped out of the boat, splashing herself as she did, getting her shorts all wet. Tony and I waited. The tall man walked over to Kekoa and stopped just before reaching her. She stood before him, quietly, with her arms at her sides. Look down at her, he put both of his hands to his lips and kissed them. Then he reached them up towards the sky and made an arch over the space between him and K. She smiled, knowingly, and so did he, and then she came into his arms for a bear-like hug. I watched in awe and looked over at Tony; he didn't say anything. I turned back to the scene on the beach; much laughing was taking place in the space that had just been blessed.

They walked up to the side of the boat and K introduced me to her uncle. She handed him our two bags, then reached out her hand for me to take. I grabbed it and then jumped. The water splashed up my legs, leaving a slight sting when the salt kissed my tiny shaving accident from the morning. Kekoa let go of my hand once I stabled myself, and then waved to Tony. He gave a slight nod before turning on the engine.

"He's not coming?" I asked.

"Nah. He just dropped us off," she said. "He'll be back tomorrow to take us home."

I followed the path leading up to the small house, and was welcomed by the sights, sounds, and smells of nature all around me. Waikiki was a whole world away; *this* was paradise. I wasn't sure where we were, exactly, but I felt safe. Hawai'i is made up of tons of little islands, and all I knew was K said this wasn't one of the main eight found on a map.

Uncle Fred's house was small. The deck we first came upon before entering the doors had been well used and was crowded with potted plants. A bamboo mat sat over to one side and two wicker chairs were on the other. If the wood had been stained, there was no trace of it now. The salty sea air stripped each plank of any color, and the breeze kept the shell chimes in constant play.

I wiped my feet on the towel by the door and carefully stepped over the walkway into the house. The living room, if you could call it that, was tiny. There was a single framed photo on a side table – a younger version of Fred and a woman laughing next to him. They were teenagers. The couch doubled as a bed, Kekoa told me, which is where she slept when she was younger.

"Now I just stay outside," she explained. Where, I wondered.

"I'll put your bags right here," Uncle Fred said as he set them down next to the wall in the hallway; his long build bent over so he could reach the floor. When he stood back upright he pointed to the photo.

"That's my dear Kiana," he said with a proud smile. "She was my first and only love." K looked happily up at her uncle.

"Yeah man, and they were *too* much," she said with a giggle. Fred grinned.

"Forty-seven years," he said. "I knew she was my beloved the first time I saw her."

"Yeah," K interrupted, clearly knowing where this story was going. "They were eight years old," she said.

"That's right," said Fred. "First love is very real. Don't let anyone convince you otherwise. And like those cranes Kekoa always folded as a kid, we were paired for all eternity."

We all smiled.

"You *keiki*, uh, kids, hungry?" Fred asked, correcting his Hawaiian for my benefit.

"We're good," said K. "I'm going down to the shop, if that's ok."

"By all means," said Fred. "Help yourself."

The shop turned out to be a glamorized tool shed, outfitted with surfboards and wax. There must have been twenty boards in there. Leaning against the wall, hidden behind a smaller board, was one painted all black. Carefully lifting the smaller board and setting it aside, K pulled out the black one and laid it across two wooden blocks.

"Wow," I told her. "I've never seen one like this before."

"I know," she nodded, proudly.

"It's very stealth," I said, watching as she began to wax it.

I took a look around the place and found newspaper clippings pinned to the wall. They were yellow and faded, but I could still make out the pictures of Uncle Fred; he was a surf legend. I came back to Kekoa and her board just as she flipped it over. There were white cuts and scratches on the backside, and a small etching of a shark in the corner.

"Mano," I heard K whisper as she ran her hand over the board. "He's here," she said.

Her movements were shaky and her face unsettled as she looked around the room.

"What's wrong?" I asked her.

"Those boards are scary," she said.

I turned and looked at them, but they seemed normal to me.

"They're fine," I replied, not sure of what was going on. K shook her head.

"No," she said. "They're scary. I think we should go."

"Ok," I said, asking no more questions, and we left.

From out of nowhere, Kekoa pulled a cigarette and lighter. She sat down on the sand right next to the shed and lit up, then tucked the lighter back into her pocket. Smoking calmed her. Looking out at the water, she exhaled slowly. I sat down next to her, without saying anything, and took in the view. We did that a lot – sat quietly and reflectively. However, I was beginning to believe our thoughts were very different. Mine were usually peaceful; hers seemed to be anything but.

I leaned back on the powdery sand and closed my eyes for a few minutes. The scent of the flowers came down from above us, and the waves alternated between a hush and a lull. I opened my eyes and sat up onto my elbows. K was still staring out to sea; her second cigarette had been lit.

"Where did you say we were going to sleep?" I asked her, recalling her comment from before about sleeping outside.

"We'll probably stay on the deck," she answered, turning to look at me. "If that's ok with you."

I shrugged my shoulders and smiled, pulling my knees up to my chest, "I think it sounds great."

"Cool," she replied, and then flicked her cigarette butt away from us.

When we returned to the house, Uncle Fred was in the kitchen cutting up fresh fruit. Papaya, pineapple, bananas and strawberries were neatly organized into four plastic tubs. A small plate of strawberries had been set out on the table for K and me to enjoy, along with two long neck glasses filled with pink guava juice on ice.

"I'm heading over in a few minutes, Kekoa," he said. "You coming this time?"

"Yeah," she said, popping a strawberry into her mouth.

I was out of the loop. "Where are we going?" I asked.

"To visit friends," Fred responded as he set down the four containers of fruit on the small wooden table. There were only two chairs, which K and I were already sitting in, so he stood. Fred reached across me and picked up a berry. He took a bite, savoring the sweetness, and winked at me.

Kekoa got up and walked over to her backpack on the floor; the miniature Hello Kitty still dangled from the zipper. She took out a plastic bag and tucked it under her arm. Fred gently picked up the fruit boxes and led the way back out onto the porch. Down the wooden steps to the left was a beat-up old pickup truck. K jumped in the open air back before I could offer to, and Fred handed her the food. He opened the cab door for me, which squeaked, and shut it with a loud bang when I was settled in. The gears were a little rusty, but Fred managed to steer us down the dirt road just fine.

It looked like we were out in the middle of nowhere. There were no paved roads, no houses or shops, and no people. Uncle Fred sensed my uneasiness, so he chimed in.

"It's quiet, isn't it?" he said. I smiled.

"Yeah, I suppose so," I said. "But it's beautiful. You've lived here a long time?" I asked.

"This is my wife's land," he told me. My eyes grew wide. "Not the whole island," he laughed, "just our home. Yeah, I've been here awhile," he said.

I grinned and nodded.

"Did Kekoa tell you where we are going?" he asked me.

"No," I replied. "But you mentioned something about seeing friends."

"The place we're about to go to is very special," he said. "It's holy ground. The people there are dear to us, and together with them with share *aloha*. Do you know about *aloha*?" he asked.

"Oh yeah," I assured him, "most definitely."

"Well, good," he said as he took a deep breath.

Fred never turned left or right. The dirt road we'd been driving on simply led up to a gate with no lock. Fred stopped the truck, Kekoa jumped out, and she swung the wide barrier open. We drove through; K closed the entrance and climbed back into the flat bed. The winding dirt road was bumpy and full of holes. I turned around to see K out the back window, her head bobbing up and down with each jerk of the truck. She never complained – not about anything, actually. Suddenly, a red building appeared, and two children with shaved heads came running out to see who'd arrived.

"Uncle Fred!" they greeted with great joy. Fred's face lit up like a Christmas tree.

"*Keiki!*" he called back as he lifted the smallest one into the air.

I helped K carry the boxes of fruit and followed her into the building. A few more children were coloring at a small communal table, and two older women in matching green and white *mu'umu'u* dresses welcomed us with broad smiles and greetings of *aloha*.

"Look who's come home," Fred said, as the two aunties took turns hugging Kekoa. It was a sweet reunion; the women's faces were aged with lines around their eyes and silver in their hair.

K put the plastic boxes on the table, and without missing a beat, the kids popped off the lids and began devouring the colorful treats inside. Papaya juice dripped down the chin of the youngest boy as the orange flesh became mush in his hand. We all laughed. Kekoa reached for a paper towel and crouched down next to him. His eyes were big and round, and his cheeks couldn't have been happier. K wiped his face and then his hands, patting him on the head when she was finished. I don't think he recognized her, but one of the older girls did. She looked about seven, and her head was also shaved.

"Hey, Anna," Kekoa gently said to her.

Anna had been shyly standing off to the side watching when we first came in. Her eyes sparkled when Kekoa said her name.

"Come meet my friend," K said, but Anna reluctantly shook her head "no." "Ok then," K said, "but you're going to miss out" – her voice rising on the end, baiting the little girl. From Kekoa's pocket she pulled a small packet of colorful paper. They were Japanese origami squares. Anna's eyes stayed glued to Kekoa, and she bit her thumb nail while watching; she so desperately wanted to come over.

Instinctively, the two aunties cleared the table and wiped it down with a cloth. Kekoa and her papers moved over to the table where the other kids were waiting. There were five children in total, including Anna. K spread the paper out, and each child took their sweet time picking out which colors they wanted. Two of them began folding squares of blue and pink, while the other two just sat there watching Kekoa. She thoughtfully showed the kids each step she did. Sometimes they followed her lead, sometime they didn't, and before long she'd made an origami crane. I used to do that, I thought to myself. But it had been a long time.

K placed her crane in the hand of the little boy and picked up another colored square. The aunties and Fred stood back, watching, and eventually Anna made her way over. She stayed close to K, and at one point I noticed Kekoa had put her arm around her, like a big sister. Anna beamed; she felt safe.

"The kids seem to love you," I said, holding a yellow square in my hands.

"We're like '*ohana*," she replied, "family. We get each other." I just listened. "The kids don't have anyone," she told me. "Their families abandoned them."

"So this is an orphanage?" I asked.

"Not exactly," K replied. "It's a HIV/AIDS center. These kids have HIV."

My stomach dropped.

I looked around the table at the sweet little faces working so hard on their cranes.

"You mean they're going to die?" I asked, panic filling my voice. Kekoa stayed calm.

"No, not most of them," she said. "They get treatment and care, but their families don't know that. They think HIV is a death sentence." She opened both hands to me in explanation. "AIDS is taboo around here," she said. "Women can't admit they passed the disease onto their children, therefore, not even admitting they have the disease themselves. The kids get abandoned 'cause no one wants to deal with it. But mostly, no one wants to be stigmatized. Some people even come here from other islands to die. They don't want anyone to know; they're too ashamed."

My heart was aching.

Kekoa looked at Anna. "The kids know it, too," she said. "Welcome to the modern day version of a colony for people with Hansen's Disease." She laughed, but I knew she wasn't trying to be funny.

"Hansen's Disease?" I asked

"Leprosy," she answered. "That's what it used to be called. Back in the day, people with the disease were hidden away on Moloka'i – much like this," she rolled her eyes. "It's important to never call someone a leper, though. It's not who they are, it's just something they have."

I'd never thought of it that way, but she was completely right. So often we're insensitive with our words, and we don't even realize it.

"Koa, look!" the littlest boy shouted, proudly presenting his folded creation on the palm of his hand. It was hard to make out what it was, exactly.

"Wow!" she said. "That's great." He beamed.

"Auntie," K called over to one of the ladies. "Where's Kai today?" Auntie paused before answering.

"Come with me, Kekoa," she said before heading outside the building. K grabbed the plastic bag she'd put on the table and looked my direction.

"I want you to meet someone really cool," Kekoa told me.

We followed the older woman down a path that led to another small building. Auntie stopped at the door before proceeding on.

"She'll be happy to see you," Auntie said to K. "It's only a matter of time now."

An overhead fan stirred the air above a frail girl who laid motionless on a thin cot. Her face was ashen and her eyes set back into her head. From the side of her mouth, dry blood sat, and her lips were chapped. Unlike the others, her hair had been allowed to grow out, but it was choppy, meaning it had been shaved at some point. She couldn't speak, and her breathing was shallow. But her eyes were open.

"Look who's come to see you," said the older woman, tenderly.

The young girl tried to say something, but was unable. That was Kekoa's cue.

"Hey," K said gently, stretching out the greeting.

Kai's sunken eyes ever so faintly twinkled. K sat down on the floor next to her and delicately touched her hand.

"I brought you something," K said with a big smile. Their eyes never let go.

K opened the plastic bag and pulled out the light blue yarn.

"I remembered," she said.

A single tear formed and fell down the cheek bone of Kai's face; her gaze still never leaving Kekoa's.

"You don't need to use it today," K continued, without losing her sincere smile for a single moment. "I'll just set it here for when you're ready," and she placed the ball of yarn on the table next to the cot. Kai managed to nod in agreement. I looked up and noticed a lone crane hanging from the ceiling above them; Kekoa had been there before.

"The first time I met Kai she was knitting a scarf," K said in my direction, looking over her shoulder, without letting go of the girl's frail hand. "Kai loves to knit," she stated with a joyful smile. Then she turned her attention back to the girl.

I stood by the door, once again in awe of the soul I'd been sharing the last few weeks with. My witness to her kindness and compassion filled my heart with such emotion it wanted to burst. I wanted to cry, but couldn't, and the lump in my throat was heavy. Quietly, I stepped back from the room, not wanting to draw attention to myself, and took a deep breath of fresh air. The scent of jasmine surrounded me.

I walked around for awhile by myself, and made my way back to the other children. Uncle Fred was gathering together the origami papers, which had managed to separate out all over the table. I helped him.

"Are you doing ok," he asked me.

"Hmm," I wasn't sure how to respond. "Why do they shave the kids' heads?" I asked instead.

"Lice," he explained with one word.

"Oh," I mouthed without making a sound.

I became startled when the second auntie walked up next to us and handed me a glass of ice water.

"Thank you for coming," she said. "It means a lot to the children. They don't get many visitors, as you can imagine." Her face was so sweet and sincere, and when she spoke her words, the lump in my throat got even bigger. "And even when guests do come," she continued, "they rarely touch the children. So," she tilted her head, slightly, "thank you." Her eyes were full of gratitude.

I bit down on my lip, trying my hardest to keep it together. But sometimes you just have to let the damn release. I turned away from the room, not wanting the kids to see me cry, and I let go. I stood there for a while, tears flowing, with the untouched glass of ice water in my hands.

Chapter 25

Kekoa had a deeper sensitivity towards others than the rest of us. She could feel things and understand people in a unique way – a way most of us couldn't. She had the ability to simply *be* with someone in a moment, and when she called upon that power of hers, beauty and light surrounded her. I saw it most evidently that day at the HIV/AIDS center; the way she was with the kids, and most especially the way she was with Kai, the older girl dying of AIDS. She was a messenger of love, *aloha*, and of peace.

One of the aunties told Fred that Kai slept better that night after we left. That was all Kekoa's doing. She helped the girl reclaim some of her dignity in her final days, and she did it while carrying a candle of hope. The girl was in much pain when we saw her, but K eased some of her discomfort by meeting her – soul to soul – in a space where Kai's body couldn't weigh her down. Watching them from the doorway, I knew they were both free and dancing together Elsewhere.

Uncle Fred's late wife, Auntie Kiana, apparently had the same *mana*, power, in her hands. She had been a *kahuna*, a healer, one schooled in the ancient ways of curing dis-ease.

"When the body is sick, it's because you are not paying attention," she was known for saying. "Dis-ease – the body *not* at ease – that's all the word means. Now," she would say with strong focus, "you must search your life, your days, the depths of your own self, to find what it is you are ignoring. Once you find it and release it, you will be well. We are each our own healer."

Kiana learned her skills from her grandfather, who most likely learned them from another relative. These sorts of gifts were usually passed down. But Kiana had never taken Kekoa on as an apprentice. K simply had her own gifts. That's not to say her Auntie and Uncle weren't huge influences on her life.

K had spent a great deal of time on their little island. Uncle Fred and K's father were as different as night and day; two brothers with contrasting lifestyles. K's parents cared mostly about money, business, and travel. Fred and Kiana, on the other hand, kept it simple and preferred the traditional ways. They took Kekoa in whenever she wanted, or needed, and she felt more like *their* child than her parents'. From a young age she saw the hands of charity and compassion at work, and when the tasks were through, Uncle Fred would take her out on his board. She loved sitting on the back as he paddled hard through the current, and he loved her as if she were his own.

Kekoa's life with her relatives was magical. Every morning Auntie Kiana would chant on the shore in front of their home, calling on the family's '*aumakua*, spiritual guide; *'au* meaning "far traveling," and *makua* meaning "ancestor." K's family believed the spirit who watched over them the most was once a part of their family and now took on the form of a shark, Mano, in the deep blue sea. When Auntie chanted on the beach before sunrise, rumor has it sharks would appear, sometimes even swimming up so close to her she could reach out her hand and pet them.

Fred and Kiana had great respect for the islands and all that lived on them and around them. Fred talked often about the *mana* in everything.

> *"There's mana in the ocean, there's mana in*
>
> *the ti leaves*
>
> *"There's mana in the people, there's mana in*
> *the breeze*
>
> *"Pikake, plumeria, kukui and maile*
>
> *"Leis of mana, Laka, dance with me,"* he

would sing while working around the house.

When I asked K about the little song, she said it was something Kiana used to sing, but now Fred was using his voice to pick up where hers had left off.

I realized, immediately, that I was in the midst of real Hawai'i. *This* was what I had hoped to experience the first time I stepped off the plane. It was nothing like the postcards and travel brochures; it was better, it was real, it was Hawai'i. Fred and Kiana carried the same spirit Auntie Mele did back home; the same as Auntie Marian and the sweet man selling shaved ice. You could *see* it in their eyes – a combination of peace and knowing. The older generation had it, but it was less common in the younger ones. Kekoa, however, was an exception.

I was beginning to see there was wisdom – deep, old wisdom – behind her words and actions. She was a brilliant combination of a wise old soul mixed with a child-like spirit. The tattoos and piercings were just a costume. And to top it off, she folded cranes. Who would have thought?

Chapter 26

The diamonds in the sky were so bright when there were no city lights to dull them. Fred, Kekoa and I sat around a small fire on the beach in front of the house. The waves had calmed by then and were rolling in gently, no longer pounding onto the sand. The island was dark, but full of sound, as the creatures of the night began their conversations.

"Some nights you can hear the spirits of the ancient *ali'i* warriors walking through the trees," Fred said, looking away from the sea and into the blackness of the island. "But I don't think they'll be traveling through tonight."

"Are you serious?" I asked. Fred thought for a moment before answering.

"What was your response earlier?" he asked. "Ah yes, most definitely!"

"You really believe all that?" I continued. "It's not just superstitions and myths?"

Fred and Kekoa looked at each other, sphinx cat grins on both their faces, and then looked back at me.

"Tell her a story, Fred," K said.

Fred nodded and poked a stick at the coals of the fire. I watched him, expectantly.

"Several years ago," Fred began, "there was a group of men traveling from this island to the one right over there (he pointed) by canoe. They were taking food to relatives on the other island. There was a big celebration about to take place: a child's first birthday. The men were bringing fish, sweets and *poi* with them in their little boat. Do you know what *poi* is?" he asked.

I nodded. I had been on the island long enough to know all about the Hawaiian staple made from ground taro and water. However, the purplish-grey paste wasn't really my thing.

"Ok, good," Fred replied and then carried on with the story. "When they were about halfway to their destination, a great shark appeared out of nowhere and swam up next to them. The shark was as big as the boat, and obviously, the men were scared. The great fish circled around them, but never tried to tip them over. Still, the men were afraid.

"In a desperate attempt to shoo the gigantic fish away, one of the men threw the *calabash* of *poi* overboard. It made a great splash, but the shark didn't leave right away. Instead, without pause, the shark moved over to where the poi floated on the water. Using its face, it pushed the poi over the waves and disappeared. Relieved, the men picked up their paddles and continued on their journey, thanking the gods who had once again protected them.

"The next day the men made the voyage again, crossing the same path of waves on their return trip. Again, they carried food with them in the small canoe; the aunties at the *luau* party had made sure of that. When the travelers reached the same middle point in their journey, the great shark once again appeared, circling the boat, gently. Recalling their good fortune from the day before, they took one basket of fish and threw it towards the giant creature, hoping it would satisfy. It did, and the shark swam way, pushing the food with its face once more.

"The men were curious about this and decided to follow the shark, but at a bit of a distance. They paddled through the waves, keeping sight of their basket. As they came upon the shoreline, they saw a small house. An old man, brown from the sun and frail from his years, was picking the basket up from the beach.

"'*Aloha*, uncle,' the men called out to the old man. 'We are thirsty travelers who have lost our way. Would you mind if we stopped here for something to drink?'

"'Please, please,' the old man said, gesturing for them to pull up their boat. 'My house is yours. Make yourselves at home.'

"The old man walked slowly, carrying the basket like a prize, and led the men into his modest home. They looked around the small space and saw he was alone.

"'You must be hungry,' the old man said, and he proceeded to serve them the fish from the basket. The men graciously accepted and began to eat.

"'This fish is very delicious,' one of the travelers remarked. 'Did you catch it this morning?' he asked, knowing full well the old man had not caught it himself. The old man began to chuckle.

"'As you can see,' the old man said, 'I am an old man. I can no longer fish for myself, but I have a friend in the cove. There is a kind shark that brings me food. Today, it even came gift wrapped in this basket.' The men all stopped eating and looked at each other.

"'Where does the shark get the food from?' another asked, wondering if the old man knew the truth. The old man smiled.

"'The gods always provide,' he said.

"For many months after, the men encountered the same shark at the half-way point of their journeys to other islands. Faithfully, they dropped bundles of food to him, knowing they would help to take care of the old man.

"One day when the men were paddling, they arrived at the mid-point destination, only to find the waves deserted. They waited and they waited, but the great fish was nowhere to be found. For three days, the same thing happened; no shark. Worried about the old man starving, the men decided to take the food to him themselves. When they arrived, they found the house empty and abandoned. The old man had died the week before, and the shark was never seen from again."

Uncle Fred poked at the fire some more with the charred stick. I looked at Kekoa. She was staring into the flames, open bottle of beer in her hand.

"That's a true story," Uncle Fred said, "and now it's time for me to go to bed." He rose to his feet and brushed the sand from his hands. "Goodnight, *keiki*," he said to both of us, and then he disappeared into the darkness.

K finished off the last of her beer and reached for her bag. She had packed it full of alcohol and soda before we left the house that evening, and was now pulling all the cans out and setting them on the sand.

"What are you looking for?" I asked.

"My pack of smokes," she said.

I reached across and snatched up a bottle of soda, suddenly feeling thirsty, when my eye caught notice of the book she'd just pulled out of her backpack. It was the same title Auntie Mele had given me for graduation.

"Hey!" I said, startled, "I have that book."

"Oh yeah?" she replied, still digging in her bag.

"Yeah," I said, continuing to be surprised. "It's not exactly something I thought you'd be interested in, though."

"Huh," she said, pulling a cigarette out of the crumpled pack she'd just found. "Why not?"

"I don't know," I stumbled on what to say. "It just doesn't seem like you."

"Looks can be deceiving," she said, lighting up. She took in a long drag and then blew out the smoke. "Turns out that's my favorite book."

"Really?!" I said, shocked. She raised her eyes at me flirtatiously.

"Yeah man," she eventually said after looking at me for a moment first. "I always carry this used copy in my bag. Makes me feel safe. There's good stuff in here."

I could tell this was going to be a night of surprises. We sat there for a few minutes while K opened another beer and moved onto her next cigarette.

"Are you planning to drink all of those?" I asked, pointing to the cans of beer she'd put back in her bag.

"Yeah, probably," she said. "But you're welcome to them, too." I nodded.

"You drink a lot," I commented.

"Don't start," she warned me before I could say anymore.

"I didn't mean anything by it," I quickly back peddled my words, "I was just surprised, that's all. You never seem drunk."

"Drinking helps my head," she said, "when it gets fuzzy." She'd mentioned something about this fuzziness before, but I didn't know what it meant. "Plus, it's the only way I can sleep," she added as an afterthought.

She was methodical in her abuse of alcohol and tobacco. She never rushed either, just simply took in one after another, and every day the ritual began again.

I decided to change the subject. Ever since going to the Buddhist temple with her, I wanted to ask questions about K's own beliefs, but the time had never felt right. Alone, under the bright stars, surrounded by nothing but the mystical darkness of the island, I felt it was safe to ask.

"Do you believe the story Fred told us just now?" I asked.

"Of course I do," she said, confidently.

"So the 'gods' in the story are Hawaiian, right?" I asked, trying to understand.

K nodded, flicking ash onto the sand.

"So then, how do you mix that with your Buddhist beliefs?" I continued.

"Easy," she said, inhaling her smoke. "It all goes back to the same place." She blew the air out of her lungs. "It's really quite simple. Just different streams leading to the same big ocean. Water is water, man, no matter how you dress it up – with salt or fish or toxins. The same is true with God."

I held my can of soda, but stopped drinking. Kekoa was shedding her physical self once again and revealing her wise soul to me. I knew to listen.

"You want to know why that book is so well read?" she asked, referring to the novel in her bag. "It's because it's so damn simple, and at the core of all of us we recognize that everything in its purest form is simple. God never made it complicated; we did."

She took in another drag of her cigarette and blew it out towards the dark sea. The fire was still burning brightly.

"It totally irritates me," she continued, "how everyone does things in the name of their idol or profit or messiah. So much of it's just crap – not all of it, but a lot of it. All these religions out there say *love* is at their cores, but then their followers act in hateful and exclusive ways. They're such hypocrites."

She snuffed out the last of the cigarette and pulled her knees up to her chest, wrapping her arms around them.

"And the really scary thing," Kekoa said, "is that they don't get it. Man, I know the Big Guy's just shaking His head. All these people who claim to be 'saved' (making quote gestures with her fingers) are the ones who are actually lost. You know what I mean?" she asked. I didn't answer or nod in agreement. I just waited for her to continue.

"They've completely missed the point. Hell, they don't even know where to find it. It sure as heck isn't in the number of hours they clock in the pew or the number of dollars they put in the offering. It's not in their dramatic insincere prayers played out for others to watch and hear, nor is it the size and number of amulets on display around their necks." She shook her head, looking into the fire. I could see this reality pained her, and then all of a sudden the rough tossing of her words calmed.

"It's right here," she pointed to her chest. "It's in here. All they have to do is look in the mirror at themselves and answer this one question honestly: *have I been a good person today*? That's all." Her face looked deflated. "Why can't people just be good people?" she asked. "That's the only thing I ever try to be."

My head cocked to the side, I looked at her – really looked – and then shook my head and smiled.

"What you don't realize," I replied, "is that what you just described is *exactly* what those idols, profits and messiahs were talking about and trying to teach." I giggled slightly out of awe. "You, my Buddhist sista, are more like Jesus than most Christians I know."

With that, she smiled.

"Why don't you hand me one of those beers," I said. "I'll drink with you."

We sat like that for awhile, and I commented on how peaceful the place was.

"You really have a hard time sleeping?" I asked. "Even here?" Kekoa paused before answering, holding back – both her words and her eyes.

"Even here," she answered. "I hear things."

"You mean like the animals?" I asked.

"No," she said, offering no more of an explanation.

"Oh," it dawned on me. "You mean like the warrior spirits your uncle was talking about."

"No, not those, either," she said. "But sometimes I think I can actually hear them, too."

I didn't understand, and my face showed my confusion. Kekoa looked at me, searching for safety in my reflection. Then she carefully placed one foot into the unknown.

"I hear things," she restated, "and sometimes I see things – things you don't see. It makes my head fuzzy, and sometimes it scares me. The drinking helps, though. It helps a lot."

The fire flickered, the flames becoming less, and I stayed still. I told myself to breathe and to not look stunned.

"I haven't always been this way," she continued. "It started in high school."

She looked at me, gauging my reaction, so I chimed in.

"Are there medications you can take, or anything?" I asked, unsure of what to say.

"Yeah man, I tried that for awhile," she answered, now more relaxed, "but I hated the way they made me feel. Well, actually, that was the problem – they *kept* me from feeling. I hated that."

"I wouldn't like that, either," I said, trying to imagine what it would be like.

I continued to ask questions into the night, and K was happy to answer them. I was the first person she had told in a long time. Her parents were too preoccupied to deal with her needs, and her uncle chose to be a safe haven for her versus someone who nagged at her to get help. I respected him for that.

A heavy burden had been lifted from her shoulders by telling me her secret, and I was honored that she chose me to reveal it to. But there was still worry in her eyes.

"Does all of this weird you out?" she asked me, holding her breath.

"Heavens, no," I reassured her. "In fact, it makes me admire you even more." I smiled. "You're an amazing soul, Kekoa. Don't let anyone – whether they are standing in front of you or inside your head – tell you otherwise. Your family named you well; you truly are *the courageous one*, and I'm proud to know you and call you my friend. Who knows," I said lastly, "I might even love you a little."

Kekoa's eyes began to tear up, which caused mine to as well. She was still holding her knees up to her chest, so I reached out my hand to her arm and gave it a little squeeze.

"Don't worry," I said. "We'll figure something out. We just have to find the right formula. The voices are in your head – not your heart – so listen from there instead," I said, pointing to her chest. "It will lead you back to the center when you're scared."

Unable to speak due to emotion, she looked at me and then moved her eyes off to the side, trying not to cry. Then she nodded in agreement.

"Do you think you can sleep tonight?" I asked her.

"Maybe," she said hopefully.

I helped her gather up the empty cans, and she covered the fire with sand. I was about to start heading back up to the house when she stopped me.

"Hey," she said, taking my hand that was down at my side.

I looked at her, unsure of where this was going. She kept looking at me and then placed her other hand over her heart.

"Thank you," she simply said, looking far into me.

"You're welcome," I replied.

The moment was there, surrounding us – soft, loving, peaceful – and then it floated away on the ocean breeze.

We climbed the steps to the deck and found two mats Fred had laid out. Kekoa surprisingly fell asleep shortly after lying down. However, I wasn't able to. My night was haunted – not by the warrior spirits, but by what I had just learned.

Chapter 27

Schizophrenia– such a long and intimidating word, but then again, so is *supercalifragilisticexpialidocious*. (You just sang it in your head – or possibly out loud – just now, didn't you?) See, we have no problem joyously celebrating the second one; society even encourages it – getting children to sing it proudly while believing in a woman who can fly with her umbrella, carries a satchel that mysteriously holds furniture, and has the ability to jump into cartoon paintings so she can twirl with penguins in tuxedoes. For some reason we don't think of *that* as being *crazy*, *insane*, *nuts, scary* or *taboo*, even though most of us have probably never danced with a large dressed up bird.

Sadly, we aren't as knowledgeable and accepting of the first word. I pray that will change one day.

Chapter 28

The waves were pounding on the shore and I was all alone when I woke up on Fred's deck the next morning. I sat up and rubbed my eyes. The sun was so bright as I looked around me, but there was no sign of Kekoa to be found. Even her mat was rolled up and put away.

"Good morning, *keiki,*" Fred called out as he walked up the steps to the deck.

"Good morning, Uncle Fred," I said. "Where's Kekoa?"

"Out there," he pointed proudly, gesturing towards the sea. "She'll be awhile," he said. "Hungry?"

Taro pancakes with macadamia nuts and fruit came out of the tiny kitchen in a matter of minutes, and Fred brought a glass of juice for himself. He handed me my plate and then sat down in one of the two chairs.

"You had quite a day yesterday, didn't you?" he asked, already knowing the answer. It seemed like a loaded question, and I wasn't sure what to say. "She's a good kid," he continued, clearly referring to Kekoa. "Don't let the shadows fool you. She's just got black bags that need healing; that's all."

I continued to quietly eat my breakfast, not saying anything.

"It's ok," said Fred, "I know she told you. She wouldn't have brought you here otherwise." He reached over and patted my knee, and then took a sip of his juice.

"Black bags?" I asked, with cheeks full of pancake.

Fred sat his glass down and crossed his hands over his chest.

"Black bags are past traumas, pains, disappointments, and failures," he began explaining. "They can be anything unhealthy or unproductive in our lives. We have a tendency to hold onto these things, and in turn they weight us down and make us sick. Our people believe the *'aumakua* and other healers, like my beloved Kiana, have the power to heal what we call *ele'eke eke*, or little black bags, from the body, mind, and spirit. True healers know the secret: most people can heal themselves, but they must completely let go in order to do so.

"Anyway," he came back to the topic of Kekoa, "she has her own black bags, and obviously they haunt her. But I also know the gods are with her

– watching over her each day. God is in the darkness, too, you know."

I thought about what he said, and then I asked the one question that wouldn't leave me.

"Uncle Fred," I asked, "how can you tell the difference between the spirit world and hallucinations?"

"That's a good question," he said "and I'm not sure I know how to answer it. But I can tell you this: Mano would never wear a leash." My eyes widened with surprise, and Fred smiled sympathetically. "I have no doubt he is with her – guiding and protecting her – but he's not the one she's walking." With that, the topic was gently closed.

Fred stood up and took the finished plate from my lap.

"It was really nice to meet you," he said. "I hope it won't be the only time, but if it is, then I'm glad we had *this*," and he headed back into the house.

I waited for K to come home, and then decided to go ahead and get ready. I knew we'd be heading back to O'ahu shortly. Eventually she came into view, paddling her board along the water's edge. She waved up at the house and smiled, and I waved in return. It was great to see her happy. She carried her board up the path and leaned it against "the shop," then climbed the deck stairs.

"The water was awesome, man," she enthusiastically reported as she sat down in the chair next to mine. Her hair was wet and dripping down her neck, and her fingers were slightly pruned from being in the salt water for so long.

"Glad to hear it," I said with a pleased expression on my face.

She caught her breath for a moment longer and then went inside to change. When she reemerged, she was wearing a black shirt with writing on both sides.

"*I know I'm in my own little world,*" the front read. "*But it's ok, they know me here,*" said the back. I busted out laughing.

"Great shirt!" I said.

"Isn't it?" Kekoa replied proudly.

There was nothing awkward between us following the previous night's conversation, and for that I was grateful.

The sound of a motorboat alerted us of Tony's arrival, and Kekoa grabbed both of our bags before I had a chance to even pick up my own.

"Aren't we going to tell your uncle goodbye?" I asked, surprised he wasn't already outside with us.

"Nah," she said. "He's gone." Confusion crossed my face. "He doesn't like goodbyes," she told me. "He probably already said it to you in his own way without you knowing." She was right; he had.

Tony wasn't any friendlier with me than he had been the day before, which I thought was humorous as we piled into the boat. Kekoa had already explained that Tony had always been a good friend to her over the years. After what she's shared with me at the fire, that was good enough for me.

K pushed the boat away from the sand and waded up to the ladder. I helped her get on board, and then tied my hair back before getting one last look of the island. Now I understood what Uncle Fred had meant when he called it *holy ground*. A part of my heart would always be there, and I prayed those who came after me would tread lightly.

When we arrived back at the condo, Kekoa walked me up to the door, carrying my bag and insisting on making sure I got in safely. As I opened the door, I saw there was a message waiting for me with my name on it. It was Auntie Mele; she was in the hospital.

Chapter 29

Kekoa insisted on taking me to the airport. I wasn't in the frame of mind to argue with her, and instead, actually appreciated the support. I knew I was rushing; my emotions were all across the map, and K's presence grounded me. She kept me calm and helped me stay level headed about what I needed to do.

Per usual, she insisted on carrying my bag for me, and even bought me a small overly priced pouch of dried coconut chips at the airport snack shop.

"You need to eat, eventually," she said, after a failed attempt to get me to eat earlier.

We stood together at the gate, quietly, until they called my flight number, and then panic started to set in. I was really about to go and do this thing, whatever it was. Kekoa must have been feeling me because she knew just what to say.

"Everything is going to be ok," she told me, "no matter what happens."

With that, she carefully put her arms around me and hugged me. It was the first and only time we held each other. We stood there for a long time, embracing, and when I finally pulled away, she touched my cheek with her finger and smiled.

"You better go," she said. I nodded; the lump in my throat weighing heavy. "Just remember to come back, ok?" My sober look broke into a smile.

"I will," I managed to say.

"Promise?" she asked sweetly, looking up at me from below the level of my eyes, like one does with a little child.

"I promise," I said, and then I walked on – Kekoa's face being the last thing I saw before boarding the plane.

PART IV

Chapter 30

"We waited for you," the nurse wanted me to know when I first arrived at the hospital. Auntie Melelani was in a great deal of pain and she couldn't breathe properly on her own. The doctors wanted to insert a breathing tube down her throat, but she had insisted they wait for me before putting her under. As I rushed to her side, I watched her frail body jerk every time someone moved her. She was hurting. I was scared to touch her, but when she saw me, her eyes lit up and she reached out her hand for me to hold.

She looked smaller, lying there under the thin sterile blanket. There were wires and tubes hooked up to a monitor over her right shoulder, and a distinctly uncomfortable odor hovered throughout the room. "Hospital smell," I thought to myself.

The doctor pulled me aside and asked me to step out into the hallway. Auntie's body was failing quickly, and he wanted to relieve her of the pain she was experiencing. He really needed to put her under. I assured him I would make my visit brief so that he could do what needed to be done. This felt like the military, and I was merely a soldier following orders. Plus, I wasn't about to cry. I pulled myself together and stoically walked back into the room.

"I got your letter," Auntie said, as I pulled a blue high-back chair closer to her bed. The letter – the one I had written to her about Jeffery – had completely slipped my mind. "Just forgive him," she said with a sweet smile, then turned her head away from me. "Time is too precious to waste on such silly nonsense." Well, that cleared that up.

"What did you do this week?" she asked me, as if we were sitting at her small table back at home and not in some bleached intensive care unit. I did my best to tell her about my recent adventures: temples and museums, Lili'u and the island, but chose not to share about Kai, the girl who was dying from AIDS. Instead, I tried to keep the conversation light. I didn't tell her much about Kekoa, either, other than mentioning her as being a good friend. Auntie listened to my tales, mostly with closed eyes, and when I was through she tilted her head back my way.

"Look at me," she said, with a sly grin on her face. I leaned in closer on the edge of my chair. The lines around her eyes curved up and a glow of subtle excitement came across her face.

"Well, bless my soul," she said with gratitude. "You've seen the face of God, haven't you?" Auntie asked in a pleased tone. She didn't wait for me to answer. "Oh yes," she closed her eyes again and smiled even wider, "you have."

A moment later the doctor returned to the room and said they couldn't wait any longer. I excused myself and left the professionals to do their work. I sat right outside the door on a window ledge looking out at Puget Sound. Mixed emotions were running all through me; I was scared about what was happening to Auntie, and I was curious about her last words to me. What did she mean I had seen the face of God? Where? Who?

A large bird flew up into the tree across the street, and there was no mistaking its white head. With a wingspan of at least five or six feet, it was none other than a bald eagle. These sacred birds were often seen around the area, and their presence always created a sense of reverence and awe. And that's when it hit me: Kekoa.

Was Auntie referring to K when she said I'd seen the face of God? Initially the statement seemed crazy, but the more I thought about it, the more it started to sink in. Hadn't I been the one to say she was much like Jesus and all those others prophets who had come before – teaching about love and compassion?

Before I was able to think too much about this, a nurse came out of Auntie's room. The nurse told me Auntie was resting comfortably now, but that she wasn't able to communicate with me anymore. She suggested I go for a walk to get some fresh air and exercise.

"Staying around here all day can be damaging to your health and your spirit," she said with a gentle smile. "Hospitals are for sick people, not for the ones who should be out there living their lives. Don't worry," she said, "I'll be right here all afternoon. Your Aunt's not going anywhere."

She was right. I hated to leave Auntie Mele, but I also knew we might be in for a long stay. The day was pleasant, with only a few clouds, and there were several places I could wander to down by the waterfront; it was just over the hill. I peeked my head around the corner of the door, saw Auntie was breathing rhythmically, and decided it was ok for me to go for a short while.

Seattle's waterfront was alive with shoppers, coffee drinkers, corporate folks, and dog walkers. Normally I would have headed right into a café without thinking twice, but right then I just didn't feel like it. The pace of the mainland was so much faster and more hurried than the islands, and people's conversations were beginning to annoy me. I just wanted to walk in peace.

I let my eyes peruse the window displays as I sauntered along the sidewalks. A handful of art stores lines themselves up, one after another, and I began to see Native American wood carvings at every turn. One particular window caught my eye and caused me to stop. In the window was a four-foot high carving – a mini totem pole, actually – with only two characters carved into it. The bottom was a female figure holding a wand of sorts, and standing on her shoulders was a bird. A few drops of rain suddenly fell on my face, and I looked up in great surprise. Where in the world did those rain clouds come from? I quickly opened the shop door to escape the downpour that was about to unleash, and was greeted by a silver-haired man who was polishing some bracelets.

"Looks like you just made it," he said, referring to the rain that was now blowing against the front windows.

"Crazy, isn't it?" I said. "I swear there were only blue skies a few minute ago."

"Hmm," the man quizzically replied. "It's not so crazy."

I left him to his polishing and walked over to the small totem pole near the glass. Running my hand over the wood, I felt the smooth ripples of the carved bird feathers, and then took the movable wand out of the woman's hand. The carving was beautiful.

"It's called *Wolf Mother*," the man said to me, now standing to my left. (Spooky – I hadn't even heard him come over.) "The woman on the bottom is holding a rattle of a Wolf. You see?" he asked, and he showed me the details up close. "Animals are very sacred to Native people. We believe each of them carries their own unique gifts and medicines. Wolf," he pointed to the Native carving on the rattle, "means 'great teacher,' and many times comes in the form of a woman." The man placed his hand higher on the totem."The bird watching over her is Eagle. Eagle represents Great Spirit. He protects her and gives her wisdom. This is a very *special* piece you have been drawn to today. Clearly, it called you in."

"Oh, I was just passing by," I assured him, feeling slightly uncomfortable about his last comment.

"Of course," he said, gently, but clearly not believing me. "Anyway," he changed the subject, "it's raining outside, and you don't seem to have an umbrella. You might as well wander around the shop and take a look until the showers let up."

I did just that. There were stunning Native masks and painted wooden carvings adorning the walls; blankets woven from black, red and white yarn piled up in the back corner; and bird feathers seemed to be everywhere. I strolled over to the jewelry case where the man was sitting; a multitude of turquoise rings and silver bracelets laid out on black felt. The man kept polishing his silver while keeping a close eye on me, but he quietly kept to his work without saying anything. Eventually he looked over his rimmed glasses at me, and paused his polishing.

"You're not from around here, are you?" he asked.

"Well, I kind of am," I replied. "But right now I'm visiting my aunt in the hospital. She's in intensive care."

"I'm sorry to hear that," he said. "She's quite special to you, I can see."

"Yeah, she is," I said, "but how could you tell that?"

"Your spirit told me," he said, matter of fact. My eyes widened. "It's the way you're carrying your spirit right now; it's heavy. Someone only hurts like that when their heart is involved. You must love your aunt a great deal."

I don't know why, but his words were revealing, exposing, and healing all at the same time. He put to voice what I was feeling, and in doing so, gave me permission to breathe. I didn't realize I'd been holding my breath the whole time until he pointed it out to me.

"You must keep breathing," he said. "When you don't know what else to do, just breathe. Just breathe." And so I did, holding on to the straps of my bag very tightly, and then I cried.

The man handed me a tissue and grinned. He was gentle, like a deer in a meadow, and his silvery hair sparkled like the stars at night. I wiped my eyes and put the tissue in my pocket.

"Thank you," I said, "and I'm sorry for losing it like that. It's just been a really long week, and I don't know what I'm supposed to do about any of it. But you're right – mostly I'm scared of losing my

Aunt. She's the most important person in my life. Everything just feels really dark right now, like there's a blackness around me. I don't know how to deal with that."

"You know," he started in, leaning over the glass top of the jewelry case, "Native people believe Great Spirit, sometimes called Great Mystery, is in the darkness. You see all this black color everywhere?" he asked, pointing to the paintings on the walls and the blankets on the floor. "Black is the color of the spirit world. It isn't a color to fear. In fact," he continued, "black is quite beautiful. It's the color of our eyes and our hair – yours and mine. Well," he chuckled, "mine was once that color anyway." I laughed a little, too.

"Black is slick and smooth," he kept explaining. "It is only against a black sky that stars can be seen or a candle can be of any use. Do not be afraid of the darkness, my friend, and remember that Great Spirit is already there."

My tears had stopped by this point, and calmness had washed over me instead. I stood before the man like a little child, listening attentively and taking in what he had to say.

"I have something for you," he said. He reached into a small plastic container of silver charms and pulled out a silver feather. "This is Eagle's feather," he said. "It will remind you to look for Great Spirit everywhere, most especially when the color before you is black." He gently reached out his arm and placed the charm in my hand.

"One more thing," he added, "I have something special for you to take to your Aunt." He walked around the front of the counter and headed to the back of the shop. When he returned, he held in his hands a bundle of dried herbs, bound in white twine. Sage, lavender, and cedar were tied tightly together, creating a very sweet scent when I leaned in to smell them. The man explained to me the purpose of *smudging*, or burning of Native herbs in order to cleanse a space of anything negative. He said it was a great way to help Auntie be at peace – releasing pain from her past, and if necessary, helping her transition into the next world.

"Just burn the end for a moment, and then fan the herbs so the smoke releases," he said. "It's best to wave the smoke over yourself and your loved ones, and then fill every corner of the room."

"I doubt they'll let me do this in the hospital," I said, disappointedly.

"You're probably right," he said, "but you can perform this medicine somewhere else and Raven, the great magical bird – who also happens to be black – will carry it to your Auntie. As long as you are breathing from your heart, the medicine will work."

I smiled. Auntie Mele would really like this man, I thought to myself.

"There's something else," he said, this time more soberly. "There's a chance your Auntie is preparing to enter the spirit world. If that's the case, there is no need to be sad. Butterfly reminds us that we each will go through many transformations throughout our lifetime, and eventually, we will shed our skin and set our spirit into flight. The little caterpillar had no idea how spectacular the view was going to be down the road. But one day its body started to tell it something; it listened, and followed where it was led. Hanging there on a branch, scared and unsure, it had to let go of everything – absolutely everything – trusting that it would be all right. That's what I call faith!" he looked at me to see if I agreed. I nodded. "Did you know a caterpillar dissolves into complete liquid inside its chrysalis before turning into a butterfly?"

I shook my head.

"It's true, he said. "And when we trust life with that kind of faith, we, too will wake up one day to find we've grown wings. We have to let some things go in order to make room for what's to come, and we have to die to our old selves in order to be reborn into the light." He waited a moment before adding his last thought. "The same might be true for your Auntie," he said. My eyes dropped to the carpet on the floor. "If that's the case," he said, "then just remember she'll always be with you, simply in a different form. That's the message Butterfly brings."

I felt I should be heading on. I thanked the man for the sage and the silver feather charm, and started walking towards the door. Just as I was about to pass the small totem one last time, I spotted two silver chains hanging on a necklace stand. Each of them had a bird pendant hanging from the bottom. Immediately, I thought of Kekoa.

"I think I'll take both of these," I said, suddenly revived.

"Ah, the pair of Cranes," replied the man as he walked over to where I was. "Those are very nice pieces." He picked them off of the stand and placed them in my hand. "Cranes have a few different meanings," he said, "depending on who you ask. They symbolize solitude and independence, but they also mean trust, connection, and love. Throughout the world, Cranes are believed to be *messengers of God*." His words confirmed what I was starting to believe to be true.

"When I was a kid," I said, "I used to fold the paper kind from Japan. I thought they represented peace and hope."

"That is also true," said the man, proudly. "Most of our beliefs, and our connections to both the physical and spiritual worlds, are universal. They can't be claimed by the boundaries of countries or religion. Great Spirit is everywhere, and always will be. Cranes are sacred no matter where you are."

The man wrapped up the two silver necklaces in a piece of handmade paper, and tied them with thin string. As he handed them to me, he looked out the window onto the busy street. The sun was once again shining, and there were no clouds to be found.

"Looks like your time here is finished," he said. I looked at the street and then back at the man, dumbfounded.

"How in the world did the weather change back so quickly?" I asked. The man just smiled over his glasses once more.

"I guess it's just what needed to happen," he said.

I was shocked. I looked back outside, in awe.

"You know something ironic?" I said. "Just before I came down here today, I saw a bald eagle fly over the church across the street from my Auntie's hospital room. Then I saw your shop before the storm started, and..." I wasn't really sure how to finish my thought. "Talk about a major coincidence," I finally concluded. The man kept grinning peacefully.

"A coincidence is simply when God chooses to remain anonymous," he said thoughtfully, and then he picked up his polishing cloth and started in on his work once more.

Chapter 31

For three days we waited. Auntie Mele's siblings began arriving from other states, and mom and dad were kind enough to stop by the hospital when they could. There was nothing any of us could do, and so we sat. Auntie was in a catatonic state, unable to communicate with any of us, and we weren't even sure if she could hear. However, the nurse assured us she could.

"Watch the monitor," she told me. "When you speak to her, the numbers rise; her heart rate goes up because she can hear you." I tried it out a few times, watching the monitor closely as I spoke, and sure enough, the numbers quickly jumped. That made me smile. It was small, but it was something.

The hours passed slowly, one after another, and it was hard to find any kind of distraction. I couldn't read, and I wasn't about to go anywhere, so I sat. I had a headache that wouldn't leave no matter what I took, and I knew what my body really needed was a good night's sleep in my own bed. Pushing two chairs together in the hospital lounge wasn't going to cut it.

I stared out the window looking over into the church courtyard next door. The sky was overcast with threats of rain, and I thought about the eagle I'd seen that first day. The old Methodist building was aging; mostly made of weathered brick and covered with moss due to the constant rain. But it also had beautiful stained glass windows on all four sides. Something about the building called to me, and I decided it would be all right to walk next door for a bit of fresh air.

I hadn't been mistaken; the church *was* old. The cold concrete steps leading up to the front were chipped and well walked on, and the handle on the door looked like it came out of medieval times. It was enormous and brass, and fit perfectly with the rest of the building.

I walked inside, which led right into the sanctuary, and took a seat in a dark wooden pew near the back. The room was vacant, except for me, and the electricity had been shut off. It was Tuesday, after all. However, the sunlight from outside shone through the stain glass, lighting up the sanctuary and bringing the pictorial windows to life. One wall portrayed a scene of Jesus guiding sheep through a picturesque valley; another was of His birth – Mary and the babe, surrounded by a choir of angels. The third window held nothing but a bountiful bouquet of white lilies, and the last joyously arranged an armful of little children sitting on Jesus' lap. The images were beautiful, and for a moment, I completely forgot about the current cross I was baring.

I had never been a church-going person, and my family only attended service once a year on Christmas Eve, so I wasn't really sure what I was doing in this sanctuary. But it was peaceful and quiet, and I had the place to myself, so I decided to stay awhile.

I watched the light change through the colors of the stained glass, and the room eventually got darker. I didn't talk to anyone the whole time I was there, nor did I pray. I just sat there, breathing – like the Native man told me to do, and I listened to my breath – like a Buddhist in meditation. When I finally decided to leave, I noticed my headache was gone.

A few sprinkles landed on my cheek just as I returned to the lobby of the hospital. Once again, I made it just in time; it seemed like my luck was turning up. The rains began to pour within a matter of moments, and I was thankful I hadn't been caught in them. Immediately, I thought of Jeffery and our soggy introduction in the condo entrance.

Jeffery – that sweet man who changed my life. Auntie was right; I was being silly with my stubbornness. Right then and there I decided I would go to see him the minute I was back in Hawai'i. The thought made my heart lighter.

The elevator reached the fourth floor and I stepped into the reception area. Auntie Mele's relatives had left to get a bite to eat, so I walked down the hallway towards her room. I didn't want her to be alone.

As I approached the door, I heard something I hadn't expected to hear. It was chanting – Hawaiian chanting – and it was coming from Auntie Mele's room. My eyes grew narrower, and I headed in to investigate. A woman I had never seen before was standing over Auntie Mele. Her long peppery hair hung well below her waist, and a single flower blossom was pinned behind her ear. Her eyes were closed as she held her hands out in front of her, palms down, over Auntie's chest. Her chant was heart breaking, even though I didn't know what it meant, and I could tell her words were full of *mana*.

I held back close to the door and looked down the hallway. I was surprised no hospital official was coming to put an end to the unfamiliar noise. There didn't seem to be a nurse or doctor anywhere. When the woman finished her chant, she remained standing for a minute longer, keeping her eyes closed as she breathed deeply. Finally she opened them and looked at me warmly.

"I know who you are," she said.

"And I think I know who you are, too," I replied. "You're Auntie Emma, aren't you? Auntie Mele's cousin from Maui."

Auntie Emma opened her arms wide and without thinking, I ran to her. I had never met this woman before, but I knew a lot about her, and at that moment, she was the most comforting embrace I could imagine. She looked like Auntie Mele.

Emma and Melelani were first cousins. Their mothers had been sisters and raised the girls together, seeing as how the babies had been born in the same month. Emma and Mele were also best friends. They went to Catholic school since their mothers were devout followers, and later strayed from the family when they wanted to delve into Hawaiian traditions.

"It was at a time when it wasn't popular to show your *Hawaiiana*." Auntie Mele once told me.

The cousins found a way to mix their Christian beliefs with their Hawaiian ones, but their parents and siblings didn't approve. It took a great deal of courage and perseverance for the two girls to continue to learn the ways of their ancestors, when even their own mothers would no longer dance the hula. Through the years, the two women stayed close, and so it was no surprise to find Emma in Auntie's room that afternoon.

"What were you chanting just then?" I asked her.

"I was calling on the gods to bring Mele peace, and I was naming our ancestors – the people from whom we came. It's time for Mele to go *home*." She said with gentle confidence.

Tears rushed to my eyes. I didn't want to lose Auntie Mele, but I didn't want to see her suffer, either. Sometimes the most loving thing we can do for someone is to the let them go.

"She's ready," Emma said. "But she needs to know you're ok." Salty drops continued to roll down my cheeks. I didn't bother wiping them. "It's time," she said again. "It's time."

I looked at Auntie Mele, hooked up to all those tubes and machines. It wasn't right; it wasn't her, and that's when I knew I could do this. I could let her go. She needed to be free.

"Ok," I softly said to Auntie Emma. "But I need to do one thing first."

I left the room and found my duffle bag in the lounge. Brushing aside the change of clothes I'd brought but hadn't used, I found the sage the Native man had given me. I knew the hospital wouldn't supply me a lighter, for obvious reasons, so I went in search of any smoker I could find.

A middle-aged man in a dark brown leather jacket was standing in the courtyard, outside the intensive care wing. His black fedora hat sat proudly on his head, with a little red feather pinned on the side. His face looked oceans away as he thoughtfully smoked his cigar. The way he did it reminded me of Kekoa. I asked if I could borrow his lighter, and he graciously handed it to me.

"I'll be just a moment with this," I said. "I want to light something over there," and I pointed to the corner of the courtyard, away from where he was standing.

"Take all the time you need," he said, and then went back to thinking deeply.

I pulled the bundle of sage and other herbs out of the bag, carefully trying not to snap the dried leaves. Tilting the sage downward, just like I had done with the incense sticks in the Buddhist temple, I lit the end and waited for the herbs to catch fire. Then I blew out the flames and watched as the smoke from the buddle went up in a great puff. The scent was musky and sweet, a strange combination, and I was at a loss for what to do next. Then I remembered what the man had said; as long as I was breathing with my heart, with *love*, the medicine would work. It didn't matter that I wasn't in the room with Auntie, nor that I didn't know the proper movements to the ritual. All that mattered was my *love* – focusing my breath from my heart to hers. The magical black bird of night, Raven, would take care of the rest. And so I breathed.

I waved the sage over me, coving my body with smoke and a little ash, and then held it out through the fence so it would rise up towards Auntie's window. While I stood there, light sprinkles began to fall again, but I didn't care; I wasn't moving. This was something I needed to do, and it couldn't wait. I figured the stars must have been crying for me.

I closed my eyes – breathing in and out – and imagined Auntie's spirit. It was white and glowing, and the smoke from my sage bundle was surrounding her. She was smiling, twirling in circles, and then she was laughing. Wave after wave, the smoke surrounded her, causing her soul to glow even brighter.

And then I heard her voice, "Everything's ok, dear one. Everything is ok."

Chapter 32

The man in the fedora was gone when I opened my eyes. The rain must have scared him away. I returned to Auntie's room just as nurses and a doctor were rushing in and out. Emma was standing along the back wall, staying out of the way, and the doctor was getting irritated. My hair was damp and frizzing, after standing in the rain, and I pulled my arms up into my sleeves to lessen the chill.

"What's going on?" I asked Auntie Emma, her face looking serious as she watched.

"She is no longer responding to the medication and the machines," Emma whispered back. "She's simply getting ready," she winked at me, "but the doctor doesn't understand that."

A few more minutes were wasted as the doctor repeated the same attempt over and over again, hoping for a different result. Finally he stopped. He left the room without saying anything to either of us, and let the nurse inform us that there was nothing more they could do.

"Yes, we understand," said Emma, poised and kind. "Thank you for all you've done."

The nurse looked at us sympathetically and nodded her head. Everyone else left.

The beeping of Auntie's monitors was slowing down, as were the numbers, and the breathing tube had already been unplugged. Emma and I stood on either side of Auntie Mele and held her hands. We didn't say anything; just stared at her face, knowing this was precious time – limited time – and that she was about to leave us.

My eyes wandered back and forth between Auntie's face and the numbers on the monitor. It was agonizing. I realized I was counting down, just waiting for this to be over; a truly bittersweet thought. The kind nurse looked at me and then switched off the sound button on the monitor. The room became quiet.

I kept rubbing Auntie's hand as the numbers slowly counted backwards on the screen; tears filled my eyes and a lump formed in my throat. These were tender minutes. Emma's face was peaceful, but her cheeks were wet as well.

In the final moments, I closed my eyes, not wanting to watch the numbers disappear. I squeezed Auntie's hand and bit my lower lip. Then I took a big deep breath and opened my eyes. She was gone.

I stood there a minute, letting the moment sink in, and I listened. The room was still. I cautiously lowered my eyes to look down at the body laid out before me, and I can honestly say Auntie was not there. It was just a shell.

I let the air out of my lungs and gently placed her hand back on the bed. Without saying anything to Emma, I stepped out of the room and headed towards the window facing the church. The cloudy sky was still dark, but the rain had stopped, and at that moment – right before my very eyes – two bright rainbows arched over the church's steeple.

Tears of emotion rushed to my face and I exploded with laughter. I couldn't stop smiling. My heart was filling up with great joy that was about to overflow. Auntie Emma came running out into the hallway to see what the commotion was about, but then stopped in her tracks when she saw what was before her. Her face beamed and her eyes grew narrow as they glowed. She walked up beside me and put her arm around my waist.

"There she goes," said Emma. "He waited for her, just as she always said he would." She smiled, and then looked down at me. "Her husband," she explained. "He was a good man, and their love was great. When he passed over, a single rainbow appeared. But today there are two," her smile stayed as she closed her eyes, savoring the moment. "They are together again – *Hi'ilawe*." With her head held high, and her eyes on the rainbows, she whispered,

"*Aloha 'oe, hoa'aloha*," she said. *Farewell to thee, my dearest friend.*

Chapter 33

A strong gale wind blew upon O'ahu throughout most of the night, but by morning, all had become calm once again. The sun was shining brightly, unaware of my sadness, and the rhythm of the island continued on as it always did. This was the day we were celebrating and saying goodbye to Auntie Melelani.

Auntie's siblings, Emma, and I all returned to Hawai'i within a few days of Auntie's passing. Emma was adamant that Mele would have a proper

Hawaiian service, and would be put to rest with her husband. There was no argument among the siblings, but for some of them it was the first time they'd returned to the islands in years. In a way, they were all *coming home*.

Before leaving Seattle, however, Auntie Emma began the sacred rituals that must be done when a loved one dies. After watching the rainbows fade back into the clouds, she placed her hand on mine and asked me if I would like to help her. She told me we had special details to tend to. I didn't know what she meant, and all she said to me in comfort was, "don't be scared."

We walked back into Auntie's hospital room, her shell of a body looking even more hollow than just a few minutes before; there was no doubt the soul had floated away. Emma wet two washcloths and handed one to me, then proceeded to wash Auntie's arms and shoulders. She invited me to do the same on the other side. Together, we bathed Auntie's body with care and tenderness, preparing her for the next leg in her journey. When we were all through, Emma removed the hospital gown Auntie had been wearing, and draped a beautiful bright cream colored *mu'umu'u* over her body. Surprisingly, I didn't flinch when trying to help pull Auntie's arms through the sleeves. Emma softly brushed Mele's hair and then walked over to her bag next to the chair. From a plastic container she pulled out a beautiful *haku lei* – flowers woven in the most exquisite of designs, and made to be worn on the head. She placed the *lei* over Auntie's forehead and down the back of her hair. Then she positioned Auntie's hands so they were resting peacefully – one over the other – on top of her chest. Quietly, we each stood back and admired. Auntie looked angelic, but even more so, she looked at peace.

Emma and I sat with Auntie Mele for some time, and eventually each of the siblings joined us. The family was quiet at first, but soon one comment lead into another, and before I knew it, they were all singing. *Kanaka WaiWai* – a beautifully harmonious song explaining how the path to God is through love, through *aloha* – floated up through the room and surrounded all of us. I felt like Auntie was among us in that moment, and joy was dancing with our sorrow.

Auntie's body was taken away after we all left that night, and her ashes were hand carried on the plane back to Hawai'i by Emma in a round wooden *calabash*. The bowl looked much like one Auntie used to have in the center of her dining room table, except this one was sealed tightly with a matching lid.

When we arrived in Honolulu, Noa was at the airport to meet me. He even had a *lei* to welcome me home with. Noa and I had never hugged before, but when he saw me he didn't hesitate. He just took me in his arms and gave me a great big bear hug, even though we were about the same build and height.

"It's good to have you back, 'eh," he said with his bright smile.

"It's good to be back," I told him.

The day of the service was bittersweet. Auntie had died, and that in itself was painful and devastating. But at the same time, she was home on the islands – with me – and boatloads of friends and family were arriving to send her off in grand style. Noa offered to spend the day at my side, which I really appreciated. I told him he didn't have to, especially since he had never even met Auntie before, but he just shook his head and laughed.

"Any Auntie of yours is an Auntie of mine," he said. "Besides," he continued, "you're part of my *'ohana*, my family and dat's just what *'ohana* does."

Noa's words meant a lot. But more importantly, his friendship meant the world to me. I remembered Auntie telling me a long time ago that blood didn't define family, nor did it dictate where one's spirit came from. I thought about the first time I walked into the Koi Café and Noa called me "sista." His kindness made me feel welcome in this new place, and I recalled thinking I was quite silly to consider him my brother. But it turns out I had been right all along.

The trees around the café were in full bloom that morning, branches heavy with fragrant flowers, and Noa helped me pick them before heading to the service. White and yellow *plumeria* layered on top of one another, forming beautiful *leis* for the day. As I strung them, I thought of Auntie, and of the first time she lifted the blossoms out of the overnight delivery box. I strung each flower with memories of her dancing in my head.

When we arrived on the shore of Lanikai beach, I was shocked to see so many boats and people gathered along the water. Outrigger canoes were lined up, one after another, with *leis* adorning their bows and paddles laying in waiting. Everyone was wearing *leis*, including Noa and I, and Auntie Emma seemed to be running the show. She was gracefully getting everyone organized when she spotted me. Her face grew into a beautiful smile and she gave me a warm embrace. I introduced her to Noa, who also hugged her, and then we released her to continue with her preparations. More guests arrived, as more *leis* were being strung, right there on the sand. Finally, the sound of the *conch* shell brought us together, and the service began.

Sweet stories were shared and tributes of hula were danced by women from Auntie's childhood, and prayers were offered up from both a *kahuna* and a minister. Auntie's siblings sang *Kanka WaiWai* once again, and lastly, Auntie Emma sang *Aloha 'Oe*, with a lone ukulele accompanying her. I recalled something Kekoa has said to me about that song. She said it was often played when someone went away, especially if they died, and that it was also very sad. Listening to Auntie Emma sing it the way she did convinced me once again that Kekoa was right. And yet, I thought the song was beautiful, even though the melody ached, just like the gathering we were all a part of.

When the service concluded, several people began gathering into the boats along the shore.

"Come with me," Noa said, as he grabbed my hand and began heading towards the boat furthest down the beach.

He helped me into the outrigger canoe and then pushed the boat out into the water with the other men. Everyone was decorated in *maile* leaf and floral *leis*, and some of the men also work black *kukui* nuts around their necks. The *leis* made them look strong.

We paddled far out to sea, heading towards the two small Mokulua islands. The twin islands sat boldly, with the sun shining down on them, as they waited our arrival. The boats gathered in the same area and sat upon the bobbing waves. Emma was in a boat a few down from ours, and she lovingly held the *calabash* of Auntie's ashes in her lap. A few of the men started chanting, with others joining in, and Emma removed the lid from the wooden bowl. She held the bowl up towards the sky and said a prayer, then very carefully poured the ashes into the water. There were tears in her eyes as she did it. When she was finished, she removed a *tuberose lei* from around her neck and tossed it into the middle of the wave that had turned grayish-white. Everyone else followed in suit; Noa and I did as well.

The water looked breathtaking – like a cloud on the waves, covered with flowers of love, all wishing Auntie a peaceful journey. The boats continued to bob on for a few more minutes, and eventually the chanting finished. The men turned the canoes around, with only their *kukui-nut leis* still around their necks, and we headed back to shore.

Noa helped me back out of the boat and we walked for a while on the powdery sand. Eventually we turned back and found Auntie Emma sitting on a rock. She was looking out towards the two islands, lost in her own thoughts.

"Now they truly are together again," she said when I sat down next to her. "We did the same thing for Mele's husband several years ago. She always said she would be reunited with him between those two islands one day, and now that day has come."

Noa and I sat with Emma as we watched the sun begin to set. It had been a long day – a difficult one – but one I think Auntie would have been pleased with. As the sky began to change color, quickly infusing with deep orange and pink, Emma looked down at the long white shell *leis* she was wearing and held them in her hands.

"These were Mele's wedding *leis*," she said.

I was surprised. Auntie had never shown them to me. Emma continued to finger the smooth shells.

"There is still a lot you don't know about her," Emma said. "But that will all come in time. We should go; the sun is ready to rest, and so should we."

Noa and I helped Auntie Emma to her feet from off the rock. Though she was a lively soul, she was no longer as limber as she once might have been. We walked hand in hand – Emma and me – with Noa slightly behind, until I came to an abrupt stop. Washing up along the sand, rocking back and forth, was one of the *leis*. Sudden panic came over me; it couldn't be a good sign. But Emma didn't seem bothered by it.

"Well, would you look at that," she smiled down at the water drenched flowers. "We believe that when a *lei* washes back up onto shore, the loved one it was meant for will one day return to the islands.

Hmmm," she murmured to herself, grinning knowingly. Then, still holding tight to my hand, she continued to walk us into the sunset.

Chapter 34

Emma was scheduled to leave for Maui the following evening. I was sad to see her go, but knew her work on Oʻahu was done and that now it was time for her to return to her home. She asked me to stop by the house where she was staying, telling me she had something to give me before she left. Noa graciously drove me to her side of the island in the early morning, and told me he would pick me up again when I was ready.

"Absolutely no hurry," he said.

"Thanks. You're the best," I replied, giving him a little smile before I got out of his truck and headed up the walkway to the home of Emma's friend.

Auntie Emma was alone in the house when I arrived. Two cups of tea were waiting to be poured on the kitchen table, and I was thankful to see we were simply using tea bags this time around. She gave me a hug upon my arrival and then gestured for me to sit down.

The long white shell *leis* she'd been wearing the day before were now arranged on the table around a bouquet of flowers, and a small white box sat next them. I reached out and touched the pearly shell *leis*, admiring their glossy shine. They didn't look like any I'd seen in the ABC stores or at the flea market; those cheaper versions were often chipping and rough to the touch, but these shells were smooth, and each one was perfectly aligned with the next.

"They're quite something, aren't they?" Emma asked, watching me admire the strands.

"I've never seen anything like them," I replied. "Didn't you say they were Auntie's wedding *leis?*" I then asked.

"That's right," she said, "and you're very observant. These aren't just any shells; these are *pupu 'o Ni'ihau*, shells from the private island of Ni'ihau. They are the rarest and most treasured of all shell *leis,*" Emma's voice continued, as if she were telling a story.

She lifted the twenty-strand white wedding *lei* from the table and draped it over my arms. The *lei* was sixty inches long, from top to bottom, and the shells were tiny. All twenty strands were joined together at the top, with one much larger shell uniting them. As I looked carefully at the detail of this intricate work of art, Emma continued her tale.

"The island of Ni'ihau is the oldest of all the Hawaiian islands, and is one of the first places where

Pele, the sacred goddess of fire, first stopped when she arrived here. Today, the island is private, and only a selected few are invited to step upon its shores. Ni'ihau is one place that is still very Hawaiian. The island itself is quite small, and lacking in the same modern comforts and green lush vegetation found here on O'ahu. But that doesn't mean it's lacking in *mana*; Ni'ihau has its own special gifts. The shells you're holding in your hand right now come from the shores of that little island, and the *lei* maker who assembled that *lei* poured many painstaking hours and a great deal of patience into it. It truly is a *lei of aloha*.

"You see these shells here," Emma said, pointing to the small pearly white ones, "ninety-nine percent of them can only be found in one place in the world: the beaches of Ni'ihau." My eyes widened. "Yes, it's true," she confirmed. "Plus, when a *lei* maker sets out to collect the shells, it's no easy task. The island has no cars or paved roads, so the people must walk a few miles from the village, bringing water, containers, and any other supplies they need for the day. Then the digging begins. Everyone helps with the gathering of the shells, even the children. If one is lucky, they will collect a small baby food jar of shells by the end of the hot day in the sun. That's just the first step.

"The shells are then taken back home and sorted. Oh, there are so many beautiful colors and shapes – they truly are hidden treasures from the sea," Emma said as she smiled with awe over the shells. "Only the flawless ones are kept, and even those often times never make it to the *lei*. Sand must be very carefully taken out of the openings, and tiny holes are pierced through the centers. If a shell breaks, it too is tossed aside. The ones who survive the process are then strung into beautiful patterns and shapes. Some are mulit-colored, and others are just white – like this *lei*," and she pointed to the one in my hands.

"That sounds like a great deal of work to go through just to string some shells," I commented.

"Yes, it is, but the *pupu 'o Ni'ihau* are sacred shells to the people of Hawai'i. For the locals of

Ni'ihau, they are a gift from Heaven – a way for the people to earn a living and share a piece of this beloved island with the rest of the world. It's their greatest form of *aloha*. For the rest of us, it's the highest form of *lei* making, and a way for us to be a part of Ni'ihau. Even the royalty of the past adored these *leis*. Queen Emma – who I'm named after – and Queen Lili'uokalani both delighted in wearing them." Emma lifted the *leis* from my hands and looked lovingly down at them.

"But it's these particular shells I wanted to talk to you about," she said. "These *leis* meant a great deal to your Auntie. She wore them proudly on her wedding day, and again on special days after. That is why I wore them yesterday at the service. One day, should you decide to marry, you are more them welcome to wear them as part of your special day." I didn't know what to say. "Only if you want to, of course," she added as an afterthought.

I told Emma I was honored, and thanked her for her kindness. I honestly couldn't imagine wearing them, but just the gesture was enough to start a lump in my throat. Then she reached for the white box and placed it in my hand.

"This one, however, I want you to have now," she said, and she cupped her hands under mine.

I opened the lid and started to cry. It was Auntie's gold bangle. *Melelani* was engraved across the front, and the carved design around the back was worn down. It had been well worn and well loved. Now I really didn't know what to say.

"I can't accept this," I managed to get out, wiping the tears from my face with my free hand. "I just can't."

"Yes," Emma very calming and firmly said, "yes you can. I know Mele would have wanted you to have it," and without waiting for me to reply, she took the bracelet from me and pushed it over my hand.

The two gold bangles laid together, clanging as I moved my arm. There was going to be no mistaking me when I came around a corner. My tears lightened up as I stared down at the two names lying next to each other.

"She will always be with you," Emma said, with a loving smile. "Always."

Chapter 35

My bracelets were making way too much noise as I tried to find the keys in my bag so I could open the condo door. Noa had stayed true to his promise, picking me up from my morning with Emma, and buying me lunch on the way back. He offered to spend the rest of the evening with me, but I just wanted to be alone. Sometimes we need our own space in order to *be*. This was one of those times.

When I finally grabbed hold of the keys, I found they were attached to a piece of string, which itself was attached to something at the bottom of the bag. When I finally got it out, I remembered – the silver Crane necklaces from Seattle. All of a sudden, the memory of Kekoa came flooding back. I had been so wrapped up in the emotions and activities surrounding Auntie Mele's death that I had somehow put Kekoa on the back burner of my mind. But now she was once again on the forefront of my thoughts, and her necklace was sitting in my hand.

When I got inside the door, I opened the little paper package and stared at the two Cranes as they hung next to each other on my fingers. The Eagle feather the Native man had given me was also tucked inside the paper, and it sparkled as I turned it in the light. I wrapped one of the necklaces back up in the paper and tied it properly with the string. The other I opened and hung around my neck, after first adding the Eagle feather so it hung right next to the Crane. I've never taken it off since.

"Tomorrow I'll go in search of Kekoa," I said to myself, "and Jeffery – I promised myself I would go see Jeffery." I had much unfinished business to attend to, but wasn't sure where to begin. "Sleep," I continued speaking out loud to no one but myself, "is a great place to start."

I tucked Kekoa's necklace back into my bag and headed off to bed.

That night I had a dream. In it, Auntie Mele was dancing. She was alive and healthy, happy and smiling, and she was wearing her long white *leis*. Her hair was wavy, let down from its usual tight bun, and there was a floral *haku lei* adorning her head.

When I awoke from the dream, I knew she was all right, wherever she was, and I knew she was watching over me. I pulled back the covers of my bed and walked barefoot to the window. The waves were lulling against the sand, and the sky was lit up with thousands upon thousands of tiny stars. This time, instead of diamonds, they looked like the tiny Ni'ihau shells of Auntie's wedding *lei*. "She's up there," I said out loud to no one in particular. "Yeah," I said, smiling and watching the sky, "she's up there."

Chapter 36

I thought Kekoa might be waiting for me at the Koi Café the next morning. She had clearly memorized my typical routine, and by now word had probably made its way through the surfers that I was back on O'ahu. But she wasn't there when I arrived in desperate need of coffee. Eddie was present and accounted for, however.

"Sorry about your Auntie, little sis," he said as he walked up to me and gave me a great big hug.

His shorts were still damp from surfing, but I didn't mind. "If you want," he said with a sly smile, "I'd be happy to have Noa make you one of my favorite Spam sandwiches. Grill up the goodness, top it off with rice, and wrap it up in *nori*. It can cure anything."

"I'm sure that is *exactly* what she needs," Noa interrupted sarcastically.

I asked Eddie if Kekoa had been out surfing with him, and she had. Huh, I thought to myself. It seemed strange to me that I hadn't seen her.

"Please let her know I'm back," I said to Eddie. He promised he would.

Back at the condo, I remembered the vow I'd made to myself – contacting Jeffery as soon as I was back in Hawai'i. Without waiting to change my mind, I wrapped my courage around me and took the lift up to his floor. When I knocked on the door, he answered, and his face lit up upon seeing me. He didn't miss a beat – quickly inviting me in and offering to heat up the water kettle for tea.

"Of course, we don't have to have tea. I just thought…. only if it's not taking too much of your time…" he cautiously backpedaled, worrying that he was being too forward. I smiled, which put him at ease.

"Tea would be lovely," I replied.

It was the first real conversation Jeffery and I had since the unfortunate incident in the hallway and the strange run in downstairs in the lobby. So much time had passed, and life had moved forward in ways I had never imagined. But it felt good to be sitting on his couch once again. It was familiar and comfortable, and his charming mannerisms and kind gestures kept a constant grin across my face all afternoon.

Jeffery followed my lead when it came to the conversation topics, careful not to overstep or delve into a subject which would have been uncomfortable for either of us. I shared with him about Auntie's passing, and he expressed his deepest sympathy. Naturally, I believed his sincerity. So many people say they're sorry when something bad happens, but more often than not it's out of ritual, not because they actually *mean* it. But with Jeffery, it was always real. I told him some about Kekoa and our recent trip to her uncle's island; he mentioned the book he'd been writing.

Throughout the afternoon, we never once talked about the incident in the hallway, and to this day we still never have. There was no need. I guess some things are best left in the past. It's not always necessary to stir everything up in order to heal it. We both knew what had happened. Why? – That answer I wasn't sure of. But as time went by, it no longer became relevant. Everyone has their reasons for why they do the things they do. Sometimes the explanations are clear, and sometimes they are hard to express. I think our break up was part of the latter.

As time went on, our relationship became stronger. It was easier to be good friends than romantic partners, and in the end, I am grateful for all the twists and turns our moments together brought. Jeffery taught me about love in a way no one else could. He showed me how to care for someone not only in the bright light of love, but also in the less joyous times. I now understand how both are required in order to complete the circle. I would have never been able to appreciate it, had I not lived it. I believe Kekoa understood this as well.

Doodling on a piece of paper later that same afternoon in the condo, a tune popped into my head. It just sort of came to me, and I started humming. Before I knew it, words were floating out of my mouth and I'd written this little song:

> *We get one trip around the circle/ life is not a dress rehearsal/ black is so damn beautiful/ and love will lead you home*
>
> *A little faith can go a long way/ dreams can come true one day/ Heaven's found in the strangest face/ and love will lead you home*
>
> *The heart doesn't give a damn/ about what makes sense or the rules of man/ so follow it the best you can/ and love will lead you home*

'Cause we get one trip around the circle/ life is not a dress rehearsal/ black is so damn beautiful/ and love will lead you home

Yeah, black is so damn beautiful/ and love will lead you home.

Chapter 37

More days passed, and still no sighting of Kekoa. I was beginning to worry; had something happened to her? Did she have a breakdown? Was she upset with me? I couldn't figure it out.

Eddie seemed to be avoiding me as well; rushing out of the café every time I arrived, making me all the more suspicious. Finally one day I managed to corner him so he couldn't leave without talking to me.

"Did you tell her I was back?" I asked him, trying not to sound perturbed.

"Yeah, sis, she knows," he said, sympathetically.

The wind knocked out of me. Kekoa knew I was back, and now she was staying away. I didn't understand. Eddie could see the sadness and confusion in my face, and instead of quietly excusing himself, he folded his hands on the table and leaned in closer to me.

"She needs to be free," he gently said, "like that fish of hers." My eyes opened wide in surprise.

"You know about the fish?" I asked, shocked.

"Yeah," he sighed, "I know about Fishy."

"It's not real, you know," I said, just making sure we were talking about the same thing.

"But it's real to *her*," he said, and then gently smiled.

He put his arm around my shoulder and gave it a little squeeze. It was the most tender moment Eddie and I had ever shared, and right then I began to understand how good of a friend he had been to both Kekoa and me. He accepted her for who she was. And, he never tried to scare me with this knowledge. Instead, he watched from a distance, with his hand outstretched to support either of us if we needed. Eddie was a good guy, and now I was beginning to really see it.

"Trust her *'aumakua* will take care of her," he said hopefully with a smile. "He hasn't let her down yet."

Before he left, I took the small paper package wrapped in string from my bag. It was the Crane necklace from Seattle.

"Please give this to Kekoa when you see her," I said.

"I will," Eddie replied, safely tucking the gift into his pocket, then pulling his hoodie up over his head. I looked outside; it had started to rain.

Chapter 38

Emma returned to O'ahu the following month, and asked if we could spend another afternoon together. Gleefully, I accepted. Being around Emma reminded me of being with Auntie Mele. Their spirits were similar, and I welcomed her comforting words of wisdom. I had written to Emma after our last meeting, and shared with her the beauty of the dream I'd had. She wrote me back, telling me she had one last item to give me.

As we sat out on the veranda of her friend's small house, the wind blew, tossing the sweet scent of *pikake* and *tuberose* to and fro. The *lei* around my neck – presented to me by Emma upon arrival – was fragrant and white, setting the stage for our conversation. Auntie Emma, of course, had a plumeria blossom pinned into her hair.

"The last time I saw you," she began, "I told you there were many things about Mele you didn't know. My hope is to share those details with you as our visits continue through the years. But today I want to talk about this."

Emma opened a small zippered pouch and pulled out a well handled rosary made of several wooden beads and a few jade ones. On the bottom hung a couple charms, too small to make out from where I was sitting. I had seen these types of prayer beads before, and understood them to be something Catholics used to pray traditional prayers with. Auntie Mele had *never* talked with me about being Catholic, other than her upbringing, and she certainly had never showed me any rosaries.

"This rosary was Mele's," Emma continued, holding it up for me to see. "I have one exactly like it in the other room with my things. I never go anywhere without it."

She handed the rosary to me, and I looked at it more closely. It was shaped like a necklace with a tail. Ten wooden beads were tied in a row, with small knots in between each, followed by one jade bead. This same pattern went all the way around five times. The circle ended – or as I later learned, began – with a tail, which was held in place by a small oval charm. The image of the Virgin Mary could still faintly be seen etched on the oval. The tail tied another jade bead, followed by three wooden ones, and a final jade one. At the very end hung the two charms, and when I look at the rosary up close I could make them out. One was an eight-pronged star, and the other was a butterfly.

"I thought rosaries had huge crosses hanging from them," I commented.

"Many of them do," Emma said. "But this one isn't quite like all the others. This one Mele made herself." I stopped looking at the beads and turned my head to give Emma my full attention.

"When Mele's husband died," she explained, "she and I decided to make rosaries as a way to deal with our grief. Keeping the hands busy can be a good thing when the mind is troubled. We picked out our own beads and began to thread the strings, tying a knot in between each one. You see this bead right here?" she asked, pointing to a slightly different colored wooden bead. "This is actually one of mine; and if you look closely on my rosary, you'll see I have one of hers. We thought it would always make us think of the other as we said our prayers." The memory made her smile.

"Anyway," she said, picking up where she'd left off, "the reason you don't see a cross on this rosary is because Mele didn't want one. She said crosses were too depressing – a sign of crucifixion, pain, suffering. In her mind, Jesus didn't come to have us focus on death. Easter is about the resurrection – *that* is what makes Him so special. So instead," Emma continued, pointing to the two small charms, "she chose to put a butterfly. It's a much better symbol of new life, don't you think?" I nodded, remembering the Native man's tale of Butterfly.

"What's the star about?" I asked, pointing to the other charm.

"Oh, that's the star from the East; the one the wise men followed in order to find the baby Jesus. Mele always loved that story," she shook her head, remembering. "The wise men – sometimes known as the three kings – were also believed to be alchemists. However you look at them, they were very unique and special people. They were magical. Mele said the wise men were a representation of God showering us with even more gifts, just when we thought all the presents had been opened. Of course she wasn't talking about material things."

"Of course," I answered.

"*Epiphany*– when the wise men arrived – and *Easter* – when Jesus rose from the ashes like a phoenix – that's what the two charms represent. And to Mele, that's what Jesus' message was about; that and love of course – unconditional love for everyone, everywhere, all the time." This was becoming a little overwhelming.

"I had no idea Auntie Mele was into all of this," I said.

"In to all of what, dear?" Emma asked.

"This – rosaries, Jesus, prayers – I don't know, all of it." I was beginning to get flustered. "I just thought she was a sweet Hawaiian woman who danced to her favorite slack key songs, made coconut pudding, and shared *aloha*."

Emma sat back in her chair and took a deep breath. Then she let it out slowly.

"Prayers are private," she said. "She probably never shared them with you because they weren't meant for you; they were meant for someone else.

Don't let these new revelations scare you, sweetie. Your Auntie is still the same person you knew her to be. But now you're learning about the depth of her, not just the breadth. What you saw was on her surface. What I'm sharing with you now was deep within her soul.

"You know how the gods of the islands watch over different things – air, water, fire, hula, prosperity, healing, etc. – well the same is true with the Catholic Patron Saints for different kinds of people and causes, or the positions of the Buddha for different days of the week, or even the animal totem spirits the Native American people have in your hometown of Seattle. They're all very similar, just different packaging – that's all. Your Auntie Mele understood all that. And most importantly, she knew her relationship with Spirit – or God, or whatever you want to call Him or Her – was a personal one. She didn't need anyone telling her how to pray or what to pray about. But she did find beauty in traditions that have been passed down for many years, and so, she made them her own. This rosary is an example of that."

The air around me seemed to be buzzing. It wasn't an uncomfortable feeling, but it was definitely different.

"Never limit God," Emma said strongly. "You have no idea what the universe might have waiting especially for you, if you'd only just be open to it." Jeffery had said something like that, too.

Emma decided we had sat long enough in the two wicker chairs, and said it would do us some good to stretch our legs.

"We'll come back to the rosary in a while," she said, and she led me down to the beach. "Let's take a walk with our feet in the water. The salt water always makes me feel better. Don't you agree?" she asked.

Together we strolled, with the wind blowing our hair, and Emma told me a few stories about her and Auntie Mele when they were younger. Surprisingly, I could picture them as young girls. She asked me about my life on O'ahu, and after we'd turned around to head back, I decided to bring up a new subject entirely.

"Auntie Emma," I began, "how does someone heal a 'black bag?'"

Emma stopped walking and turned towards me. Her face was no longer light and carefree. It was more serious now.

"You know a lot more about being Hawaiian than I thought you did," she replied. "Black bags are heavy things, and each person's are unique – just like our prayers. Are you talking about your own black bags, or are you referring to someone else's?" she asked.

"I have this friend…" I started in, and then I wasn't sure how to continue.

Emma paused thoughtfully for a moment before saying anything. She looked out at the ocean, possibly searching for the right words, and then turned back my way.

"Be careful about carrying the burdens of others," she said. "Before you know it, they might become your own. It's a noble thing to help someone in need, but we must always remember to set boundaries. We've each been put on this earth for a special reason, and we each have our own journey to walk. It would be a shame to take that away from another, just as you would never want anyone to rob you of your path.

"There are two things you *can* do, however. The first is a type of cleansing, an offering of sorts, that you conduct in honor of your friend. Take a piece of paper and write down everything that's weighing her down – at least the things you know about. Then burn the paper in a tin can. Let it burn until there is nothing more. The smoke will most likely be thick and black, but don't let that scare you. This is a good thing. The smoke will release the pain and heaviness, the toxins and disappointments, all of which is heavy and dark. When the ashes have cooled, notice what little paper is left in the bottom of the can – it won't be much. That's the soot, the small remnants we often hold onto, even when we know we shouldn't. Take the burnt flakes to the sea and wash them away, using the salt water to cleanse and refill the container. This is the *kailani*, the heavenly sea, the living water. From it is where we came, and one day to it we will return. The sea is stronger and larger than anything else on this earth," Auntie concluded, "except for one thing."

"What's that?" I asked, hanging onto her every word.

"*Love*," she simple said. "Nothing is stronger than Love. And *that* is the second thing you can do; you can love her. Send her all the Love, Peace, and Healing your heart can muster up. Trust the ocean breeze to carry it where it's meant to go, and believe in the Mystery that is beyond all our understandings, but which is very Real.

"If you do these things, your heart will be calm, and maybe, just maybe, your friend's will be too. What have you got to lose?"

Chapter 39

We returned to the house and I sat down under the shade of the small banyan tree. Auntie Emma returned from her bedroom carrying the rosary that matched Auntie Mele's. She laid them next to each other and then took a sip of tea. Both strands of beads were old and worn, and I could see where the two special beads had been swapped by the girls; they really were twin rosaries. But all of these gifts were becoming too much, and I was starting to feel uncomfortable about receiving them.

"Auntie Emma," I started in, "I really appreciate what you've been trying to do – giving me Mele's treasured items and all. But I have to tell you, I don't feel right about it."

"Whatever are you talking about?" she asked, sincerely confused.

"I mean, I'm not Mele's granddaughter or niece, and I'm not even Hawaiian, so I don't understand why these things are being given to *me*." She tilted her head back in a nod. Now she understood.

"I see," she said. "There are two reasons, and two reasons only, why I have given them to you. The first is because Mele loved you very much, and I know this is what she would have wanted. And the second is because if we don't pass down the traditions, treasures, stories, beliefs and wisdom of our ancestors, it will be lost forever. We can't have that, now can we?" I quietly shook my head in agreement. "You're right; you don't have a single drop of Hawaiian blood running through your veins. This is true. But your spirit is from these islands, girl. I can see it, and Mele saw it too.

"So, if there's nothing else, I'd like to show you how to use this," and she picked up the two rosaries, putting one in my hand and one in hers. She and Auntie really were a lot alike, and I had to chuckle.

"What I'm about to show you can't be found in any book, mainly because we wrote it," Emma laughed, seeming quite proud of herself as she said it. "More truthfully, Mele and I worked on it together, crafting it over the years. This meditation, or prayer, or whatever you want to call it, is something Mele and I practiced every day – and I still do now. If I don't, my day doesn't turn out right; instead, everything feels off. But by doing this, I can plug into the Great Mystery surrounding us, and *that* is why I am usually quite pleased with life." Emma smiled and tossed up her hands, careful not to drop the rosary.

"Ok then," she said, "follow me and I'll walk you through the beads. The first thing I always do is center myself." She put the palms of her hands together – much like the way Kekoa did in the temple – and wrapped the beads around them, with the tail safely tucked inside her palms. She closed her eyes and placed her hands in front of her face, then dropped them to the level of her chest. Softly she breathed in and out, and then she opened her eyes. I tried to follow her lead.

"I *was* raised Catholic," she reminded me, "so a few things I have kept the same. I always start by imagining, or holding, the star and butterfly, and then I invite the spirits.

First I invite God – or Great Spirit, Great Mystery – whatever name you're comfortable with; then I call upon Mary – the feminine spirit, the mother, the chosen one, the woman who was asked to believe in a time when it was crazy to do so; and lastly I call on the child. That could be Jesus – a holy man who was considered a rebel in his time; or Buddha – a human prince who renounced his birthright to live simply in order to reach enlightenment, also a rebel;

or the *ali'i*, sacred royals who led our people; or even just us – for we are all children of God.

"Then I move onto the first bead. This is where I state what I believe. Again, we originally borrowed some of this from the Catholic tradition, but over the years it has evolved to a place where I feel the closest to Spirit:

> *"I believe in God the Father* (or you could say Mother,) *who is Almighty and the Creator of the Heavens and the Earth.*
>
> *"I believe in his Son, who was conceived by the Holy Spirit, born of the Virgin Mary, lived and taught a life of Truth and Love, suffered, was crucified, died and was buried. It was hell. On the third day, He arose and now sits next to God the Father* (or you could say Mother,) *where he embraces the living and the dead.*
>
> *"I believe in the Holy Spirit* (the Spirit that surrounds all of us,) *in the Holy Church*

(which is any person or group of people living their lives from a place of Love,) *in the Communion of us All* (the gathering of people in the name of Love,) *in Resurrection* (anytime anyone rises from the ashes), *and in Life Everlasting* (knowing our spirits will live on forever.) *Amen."*

"Amen," I said.

"The next bead is The Lord's Prayer," Emma explained. "And like I said before, Mele and I loved tradition, and honestly, this prayer is pretty perfect just as it is. Shall we give it a try?" she ask. I nodded, and Emma began again.

> *"Our Father who art in Heaven, hallowed be thy Name.* (This simply calls on God and recognizes Him, or Her, to be Holy.)
>
> *"Thy Kingdom come, Thy will be done, on Earth as it is in Heaven.* (This is our hope for the future; that Earth will be as glorious as what we perceive Heaven to be.)

"Give us this day our Daily Bread (take care of our needs), *and Forgive us our trespasses as we Forgive those who trespass against us* (help us learn to forgive ourselves and others).

"Lead us not into temptation, but deliver us from evil (keep us wise and safe).

"For Thine is the Kingdom, and the Power, and the Glory forever (Paradise, Power and Glory are not man made, but from Elsewhere.) *Amen."*

"Amen," I said again.

"You doing ok?" Emma asked before moving on any further.

"Yeah, I'm ok," I told her. "I especially like that you're explaining all this stuff to me. These prayers used to sound old, stuffy, and a little scary before, but now they are beginning to feel more universal."

"Oh, I'm so glad to hear that," Emma said, her face lighting up. "Let's keep going.

"The next three wooden beads are prayers for others. This is where we call on the healing embrace of any spirit you like to comfort those in need. The first bead is for all those who are suffering *physically* from health, illness, violence or imprisonment. Sometimes I have certain friends in mind, and other days I simply put the prayer out there for whoever might be in need.

> *"Hail child, full of Grace, God is with thee* (or whoever you want to call on.)

"The second bead is for all those who are suffering *mentally*. Perhaps they suffer from stress, mental health, addiction, verbal abuse, or discrimination."

Immediately I thought of Kekoa; this was her bead.

> *"Hail child, full of Grace,"* Emma continued. *"God is with thee.*

"And the third bead is for all those who suffer *emotionally* and *spiritually*. This includes heartache, loss, emptiness, depression, fear, and anger. I also include a special moment of silence for mothers who've lost children. That's a black bag no woman should ever have to carry.

"Hail child, full of Grace, God is with thee.

"Now we start to focus inward on ourselves," Emma said. "And we start with one of my favorite pieces of scripture from 1 Chronicles. It's a simple blessing for each day. It goes like this:

> *"And she called upon God saying, 'Oh please, Bless me <u>indeed</u>* (which is just a fancy way of saying greatly), *enlarge my territory* (which means she wanted to touch the lives of many), *steady me with Your hand* (asking God to stay by her side and to inspire her), *and keep me from harm.' And so, God granted her request.*

"I've always loved that," Auntie Emma said, quite pleased sounding. "It's so simple, and yet it takes care of everything you really need to ask for."

"Yeah," I replied, "I have to say it does. I don't know much about scripture, but I do like that little story."

"That's why Jesus told stories," Auntie said, "so *everyone* could understand. It saddens me that academics and scholarly religious types have forgotten that. Anyway, where were we? Oh yes, moving right along; the next jade bead.

"Each time we come to a jade bead, we have to celebrate the theme we're about to focus on. Sometimes I hum a bit of a Hawaiian melody, sometimes part of a church song, like *Glory Be*. It doesn't matter what you chose, just imagine something you enjoy and sing it – either out loud or in your head.

"The first theme, then, is **Truth**, and its color is blue – like the sky. Close your eyes and focus on it.

Truth means God is All Powerful; every good thing comes from God. God is loving, equally, towards All, and He does not abandon. God comes in many names and many faces, and He is inside each of us. There is nothing to fear – there never has been and there never will be. Sometimes difficulty surrounds us in order to get to Truth, but Truth will always prevail. It is the reason we Hope because nothing can destroy it. Like a beacon, its Light shines forever. Truth.

"Then we move onto the next ten wooden beads, saying the same prayer each time. I imagine Mary gently putting her hand on my shoulder and saying these words:

> *"Hail child, full of Grace, God is with thee. Blessed are thee among women, and blessed is the fruit of thy womb.* (Simply meaning that *everyone* is special and anything we create out of love will be blessed.)

"I, in turn, answer her by saying,

"Holy Mary, mother of God, be with us now and at the hour of our need. Amen."

I do that for each of the ten beads. By the time I have reached the last bead, I'm usually quite peaceful.

"The second theme is ***Joy*** – yellow like the bright sun. After humming my little tune, I focus on what Joy is all about. It's finding Light everywhere – in the small and significant moments of each day; and Gratitude for so many Blessings. Joy is laughter, smiles, embraces; nature, words, art, dance, song, food, creativity, and passion! It's being thankful for another day of living, and being a reflection of Spirit both inside and out. Joy means keeping a positive frame of mind and a clean heart. Joy.

"The ten beads that follow Joy are your dreams. If you haven't done this already, you should sit down some afternoon and make a list of everything you ever want to do in your life – no matter how big or how small. Pick the top ten items on your list and assign each of them a bead. When you hold those dreams between your fingers, close your eyes and imagine you are already there. Feel them, see them, and picture the people who join you; *live the dreams*. I promise you, if you love those ten little beads with all the passion you can find, they *will* come to be. Maybe not exactly in the way you imagine – or in the timing you hoped for – but they will find their way to you. If you do all of that and they still never come, then they were never your dreams to begin with. They were probably someone else's. Not to worry, though; it just means something more ideal is waiting for you."

This was starting to sound like a ton of work. I couldn't imagine doing all of this *every day*. But as we continued to move along the rosary, I became more and more comfortable with Auntie's way of seeing the world, and I had to admit, she had some great words of wisdom.

"Alrighty," Auntie said, "we've stated what is True, celebrated that which is Joyful, and now we move onto the soft white light of ***Love***, which is the third theme. This bead glows, literally," she said.

"because God is Love, we are Love, and the core of our beings is nothing but pure Love. Loving means being the face of God *for* others and recognizing the face of God *in* others. It's being kind and compassionate to everyone, and helping people carry their burdens. A place of Love is the purest place we can know; it's the purest emotion we can feel, the one true connection and true union. Love is the opposite of fear, and the only thing that's Real. Love.

"For these ten beads, I send love to people I know. Some days I use all ten on the same person, and some days it's ten different people, or a group of people. Whatever you feel in your heart that day is the right thing to do. You can't mess up prayer. As I think of each person I say,

"Hail child, full of Grace, God is with you."

"The forth theme is a little difficult sometimes. It's the color of a garden, which stands for **Forgiveness**. Remember that others know not what they do. When someone lashes out, it is because of their own pain and fear; the same is true for us.

Refrain from hurting others with negative thoughts, words, or deeds. Remember that some things must die in order for new life to be born. And be rest assured, if someone is lost, they will always be found. Be gentle with yourself, and with others, and pour Love over the darkness; it's the one thing that heals all. Forgiveness.

"The wooden beads that follow are for the people who have hurt you. You don't have to say or pray anything, if you don't want. Just simply be with them.

"And lastly, we come to ***Peace***. After humming your little tune for the fifth time, imagine the color of lavender fields. Know that the Grace of the Holy Spirit is always surrounding you; the natural state of your being is Calm. You will know what to do, when to do it, and how to accomplish it; trust, and help will always come. If need be, you will know when it's time to move on. Nature, the seasons, the ocean, the stars – one with the rhythm of Earth and Heaven. Never forget you can *always* rest in the safety of God's gentle hands. Peace.

"As you close the circle, hear Mary's voice saying *'God is with thee'* for each of the last ten beads, and end with a final little bit of humming.

"Amen," Emma concluded.

"Amen," I echoed.

She dropped her hands back into her lap and took a few deep breaths.

"Thank you," I said, "for everything."

Emma placed her rosary in her lap and cupped my face with both of her hands, looking deeply into my eyes.

"You are most welcome, my dear," she replied.

We smiled at each other, and we each let out a long breath. Then she pulled my face towards her and every so gently kissed my forehead. I sat back from her embrace and must have looked exhausted.

"You look tired, dear. Was all of that too much?" she asked, "because if it was, there's a much simpler way to do it." My eyes widened out of curiosity.

"You just take two deep breaths. On the inhale of the first, imagine these three things: peacefulness, a state of calm, and safety. On the exhale, release any toxins, anger, or fear that are sitting on the surface. On the second inhale, imagine a cleansing, healing breath coming in to fill you; and on the exhale, *smile*. Don't imagine the smile, actually do it. That's all," she laughed, shrugging her shoulders.

"That's it?" I asked, a bit skeptical.

"Yep, that's it," she replied. "Of course you could take more breaths, repeating the same process, and you're bound to get better results. But for the most part, that's all there is to it. Remember, life is quite simple, and God has a great sense of humor. If He didn't, we'd all be in trouble." And with that she let out a great laugh from the depth of her soul; it was *aloha* and *mana* combined.

Chapter 40

That same night I had a vivid dream. I was walking through the most magnificent garden imaginable. The grounds covered acres of land, with lush mountains and streaming waterfalls draping the background. The bright sun, reflecting off the rocks and dew drops, caused diamonds of light to sparkle near my feet, and flowers of every color bloomed in abundance. Hawks, eagles, ravens and cranes soared overhead, and butterflies fluttered near the ground.

The breeze was soft and fragrant, with a touch of mystery swirled in. Without seeing them, I could *feel* the spirits of the Hawaiian gods protecting the Native American animals, and from the light blue sky, I *saw* Auntie Melelani and Kai – the girl who died of AIDS – watching over. They were healthy and whole, and their eyes told me they clearly knew a secret I wasn't privy too quite yet. Queen Lili'u was there as well, smiling proudly.

Off in the distance I saw two figures sitting together in a meadow of daisies. Jesus and Buddha were laughing together like old friends; they were brothers.

Of course, I thought to myself – of course they are.

When I turned around, a woman in a flowing cream dress walked past me. She was surrounded by creatures of the forest – deer, wolves, squires, and a bear. There were flowers in her hair and a *lei* of origami cranes draped over her hand. It was Mary; the maternal figure of gentleness and compassion. As she came to the place where I was standing, she held the *lei* out to me. I reached for it, and all at once the delicate folded papers tore away from the string and transformed into real birds. They flew higher and higher, every which way, and their colors kept changing into all the hues of the rainbow. Mary didn't say a word; she just nodded in my direction, and then continued on to where the brothers were waiting for her among the yellow flowers.

Everything was right in the world; everything was peaceful and free. Life was interwoven, and somehow it all made sense. I didn't know how to explain it, but I just *knew*. And as I watched myself come to this realization, I looked up; Great Spirit was grinning.

Chapter 41

With a pack of three-inch square silver foil papers, I sat down cross-legged on the floor of the condo. Between my time with Auntie Emma and the dream that followed, I now knew what I needed to do. I had to find my own way to let go, and this was it.

Relying only once on the small instruction sheet at the back of the package, I began folding origami cranes. The first few were just for practice, and I figured I'd probably end up throwing them away. The silver foil, though striking to look at, was less forgiving than regular paper. But then, as if Auntie Mele was speaking in my head, I knew I couldn't toss any.

"Every crane is beautiful in its own way" I heard her say. "And each deserves to be honored."

I folded and folded until the ends of my fingers began to dry out. Surprisingly, I didn't get a single paper cut. When I had enough cranes for what I needed to do, I cut a long piece of string. I threaded the small needle that had come in my miniature sewing kit, and pierced the first crane – going in through the right side and out through the left – and then pulling the thread halfway through. I opened the wings of the crane and held the two pieces of thread out to the sides. The crane floated there in mid-air – in the center of the string – beautifully.

I began opening all the other little cranes which had piled themselves around me, and lined them up in perfect little rows – twenty cranes in each. Taking a small silver bead from the plastic bag they came in, I dropped a round ball onto the needle, and then the first crane.

One after another, I strung a bead and then a crane. When the first side was finished, I did the same for the other. It took some time, and a few silver beads ended up bouncing away until they found shelter under the sofa. But in the end, after tying the ends of the strings and making a bow, I was quite pleased with my creation. I had made a crane *lei*.

I hung it on the edge of the sofa, smiling at the finished product, and then started in again with another square of paper.

"Triangle, triangle, square," I began, making the first folds that would be the foundation for the rest. "Ice cream cone, then open the shutters," I continued, having made little names to help me remember the steps. "Lift, poke and fold in," came next, ultimately leading to "the kite," and then "the canoe."

"Fat legs to skinny legs," I chuckled, making the two pieces dance before turning them up to become the neck and tail. And then I folded down the head and opened the wings.

Sitting before me in the palm of my hand was the same little crane shape the children on the island had made; it was the same thing that hung above Kai's deathbed, and the same little bird I used to make when I was a child and ever so cleverly put into the *lei* Auntie kept all those years ago.

The Crane – a symbol of peace and hope, healing and love; a messenger of God, and a reminder to me of all that my life had become.

I touched the two charms hanging from my silver necklace – the Eagle feather and the Crane – and then went back to work. I had a second *lei* to finish.

The next morning I took the bus back over to 'Iolani Palace and walked alone through the trees leading to Queen Lili'u's statue. There were no *leis* hanging from her hands this time, but there was a little butterfly perched on her shoulder. Maybe it was actually a moth, I'm not really sure, but I chose to see it the way I wanted to.

I looked at the two *leis* in my hand – one for Auntie Mele and one for Kekoa. Each had been folded and strung in love. The beads were the prayers – for healing and peace – and the cranes were the beauty that came out of those prayers. The crane on the bottom was the Spirit piece, carrying *aloha* and *mana* where it needed to go. The only person I knew to leave them with was Lili'u.

I draped both *leis* over the Queen's arm, and immediately the winged creature took to flight. For some reason that made me laugh. I figured Auntie Mele and Queen Lili'u were probably off having tea together somewhere.

"You two girls have fun now," I said out loud, not caring if anyone heard me. "And please watch over my friend," I added. "She's got a good heart, but her head is troubled, and I don't know what else I can do."

A light breeze picked up, and the faint scent of *tuberose* once again surrounded me. I have no idea where it came from, but I took the heavenly perfume as a sign that my request had been heard, and then the last words Kekoa said to me rang in my ears.

"Everything is going to be ok," she had said, "no matter what happens."

I desperately wanted to believe her.

PART V

Chapter 42

Time has passed, and I'm still surprised I haven't seen much of Kekoa. I saw her once several months ago. Actually, I saw her truck first; it was parked outside a pool hall. When I realized it was hers, my heart skipped a beat. I looked inside the cab and caught a glimpse of the silver crane necklace I'd asked Eddie to give to her. It was hanging from the rear-view mirror, which made me smile. It was a sign of hope; she hadn't forgotten.

When I found her in the hall, she was smoking in the back corner, still sporting dark shades and a black shirt. Her hair was longer, and I noticed a new tattoo on her forearm.

"Hey," I called out, excited to see her.

"Hey," she said back, cordially, but that was it. It was like she hardly knew who I was.

I've come to understand this behavior is typical of people carrying the same types of black bags as she has. I tried not to take it personally, but it was hard not to. She had been my friend, my sister, and one of the most beautiful souls to ever cross my path. She was bursting with the *aloha spirit*, but she didn't know it – and I missed her.

Kekoa was the most *real* person I'd ever known; more real than my parents, Jeffery, or even Auntie Mele and Auntie Emma. She always said what she felt, with no excuse or apology, and she never lied. I don't think she knew how.

She was funny, refreshing, wise and compassionate. The piercings, ink, and dark clothes were just a cover – a mask. They helped her hide from the shadows that scared and haunted her, and they also helped her *feel* when she was unsure of her reality. She desperately wanted to *feel*, but she lived in a world of extremes; one where her senses were either too strong or non-existent. There was no balance; there was hardly ever any peace. And yet she never took the easy road out. Instead, she kept on. *Courageous One* – her family named her well.

I want to believe there is a moment – the one when she first wakes up – that is terror-free. I want to believe that in all the madness and uncertainty that life throws at us, Grace comes blowing in from time to time. Maybe life *isn't* easy – more so for some than for others – but I stand with K; I'd rather *feel* than not. To dull the pain means having to dull the joy as well, and I think both of us would rather live our lives with all the colors of the spectrum, not just the earth tones.

I don't have a photo or any special memento from our time together, but I do have that small piece of light blue yarn that somehow managed to make its way to the bottom of my bag. I take it out every once in a while, and I recall a time when a strange and glorious window to the universe seemed to open up for me. Kekoa showed me a world I would have never found on my own, and she gave me permission to find my own way in life – one free of judgment or rules. In a way, I believe she *was* the face of God, and her message was simple: *we should all just be good people.*

I still pray for Kekoa every day, but I no longer look for her. We each have our own paths to follow, and if Raven's magic truly works, ours will cross again one day. Or perhaps, she was simply like the lines of an old country song; a wounded angel flying too close to the ground.

Every now and again the guys talk about a great white sighting off the tip of the island, and I imagine K might be paddling her board next to the magnificent fish. But Eddie hasn't seen her or heard from her in months, and he says this time it's been longer than usual.

"Trust her *'aumakua*," he once told me. That's all I *can* do; she's in God's hands now.

I'm no longer scared of sharks like I used to be, and just recently walked out into the waves at dawn. When the water was up to my chest, I let myself go and dove under. Free and comforted, I surrounded myself with the warmth of the flowing waves. I was swimming with Auntie Mele, and who knows, maybe Mano was close by, too. I could taste the salt on my lips, and when I extended my foot all the way down, soft sand melted under my touch. My body bobbed with the rhythm of the waves as the sun slowly began to come up from below the horizon. I was one with the sea.

When I came out of the water, I wrapped myself in a towel and sat on the sand. Far out from shore, patiently waiting for the next big wave, were the guys who'd been my friends and confidants. They were my *'ohana*. Auntie was right, blood doesn't define family – spirit does. In the last place I thought to look, I found the security I needed.

While the sun grew brighter and began to warm up the morning, I looked around me at the tourists already planting themselves on the beach. Men, women, gay, straight, Buddhist, Christian, schizophrenic, alcoholic, infected, divorced – all just a bunch of labels; boxes that we put ourselves and others in without even realizing it. Why do we do that? Why is it even necessary? I looked back out at the sea; the answer once again made simple. The ocean laps itself upon the shores of every continent; it opens its arms to every being; and it's always going to be there, no matter what. The ocean will never discriminate, and neither should we.

My journey has taught me many things. It showed me that love is everything poets said it would be… and more. But the most important thing I learned is this: that which is *Real* is felt with the heart, not seen with the eyes. And the mind, though sometimes deceptive, has the ability to create beauty in the madness. There's a fine line between genius and insanity, and that line dips to one side or the other now and again.

So bring on the visions, the hallucinations, and the dreams. For somewhere in the middle where they meet – in the strange and magnificent center – Truth, Joy, Hope and Love all merge together as the sun shining over the day, and Peace acts as the moon. *This* is Elsewhere, the place where God resides, and I know now that He is smiling.

When the guys returned to shore, I decided to make two bold moves.

"Hey Eddie," I called out as he walked up towards me, board in toe. "I think it's time I try some of that Spam of yours. What do you think?"

"Woo wee! You got it sista!" exclaimed Eddie with great joy. Noa shook his head and laughed. I had come *home*.

Chapter 43

"Ok, you guys," I said as we were all piled into the truck on our way to the airport. "Be nice and please don't embarrass me."

"Don't worry, little sis," Eddie said with a mischievous smile on his face. "We'z just so excited to finally meet S-A-M," he spelled out Sam's name with great emphasis.

The second move I decided to make was to contact my first love – the childhood crush that never really went away – with the hope of meeting up in either Seattle or Hawai'i. With a beautiful *tuberose lei* in hand, I waited with the boys at the gate entrance. Unlike my first trip to the islands, when the *leis* were nowhere to be found, I wanted Sam's to be extra special. I was now part of the community on O'ahu, and like I had promised Auntie Marian, I would share *aloha* whenever I could.

As passengers began getting off the plane, tiny butterflies started dancing around my stomach. Just breathe, I kept telling myself. Just breathe.

The boys were cracking jokes with each other, clearly getting excited for the big introduction, and I turned around to give them a look when I heard a familiar voice call out my name.

"Sophia!"

I spun around immediately; a huge smile planted on both of our faces. Within moments we were inches apart and I presented Sam with the *lei*, who seemed quite touched. We walked over to where the boys were standing, and the look on their faces was priceless.

"Are you going to say it, or should I?" Eddie asked Noa and Jay.

"Go for it, dude," Noa replied. I just kept smiling, with laughter soon on its way.

"Sam's a girl!" Eddied shouted out in great surprise.

"Yeah," Sam answered him with a bit of a chuckle, "I am. I get that a lot; Sam is short for Samantha."

I didn't say anything, but this time it was me who had the mischievous grin on my face. Everyone just stood quiet for a moment. Then Eddie broke the ice.

"Well, cool!" he said. "Works for me," and we all let out a round of laughter. Eddie walked over to Sam and took her bag, putting his arm around her shoulder. "Come this way, sista. Your chariot awaits."

"Oh yeah," Noa said sarcastically, as he, Jay and I walked behind them. "Some chariot."

"Do you mind?" Eddie shot back at Noa, trying not to laugh. "Now *Samantha*," Eddie said, drawing out her name; the rest of us rolled our eyes. "There's just one thing I'm dying to know."

I held my breath, not sure where this was going; Noa put his arm around me in support. Eddie turned back and winked at me before he carried on.

"Sam," he started in, "how do you feel about Spam?"

Epilogue

I wiggled my toes so sand could slip between them. Warmth from the sun kissed my skin, and the ocean rocked back and forth like a lullaby. As I stood looking out at the horizon that must surly lead to Elsewhere, a gentle hand squeezed mine. I tilted my head slightly to the side and smiled. Once again, Auntie Mele was right – the treasure for which we truly seek usually comes in the package we least expect. I sat down on the sand and leaned back; the breeze blowing just enough to move the charms on my necklace and feather my hair. Nearby, a guitar started in, this time playing *Hi'ilawe*, and I laughed at the bizarre brilliance of it all.

And later that day, somewhere along the water's edge, a local *kahuna* watched. He waited as a girl in black stood out on the coral reef a ways from shore. A great white shark was circling around her as she was leaning down to pet it. When the *kahuna* was later asked why he didn't step in to stop the girl, he smiled and simply replied, "Because there was no need; God was standing beside her."

Maria Simon has spent the last 20 years teaching, counseling, and empowering young adults through universities, leadership programs and spiritual retreats. Since 1993, she has volunteered countless hours for Rotary International, Chrysalis International, and other non-profit groups who aim to make a responsible difference in the world – acting as a motivational speaker, program coordinator, event planner, and international ambassador. She currently teaches at Mahidol University International College and resides in both the Pacific Northwest and Southeast Asia. This is her first novel.

www.maria-simon.net

facebook.com/Ill-Always-Walk-Your-Fish-with-You

7210378R00244

Made in the USA
San Bernardino, CA
27 December 2013